Goldwin Smith, William Alexander Foster

Canada First: A Memorial of the Late William A. Foster, Q. C.

Goldwin Smith, William Alexander Foster

Canada First: A Memorial of the Late William A. Foster, Q. C.

ISBN/EAN: 9783337190477

Printed in Europe, USA, Canada, Australia, Japan

Cover: Foto ©Raphael Reischuk / pixelio.de

More available books at **www.hansebooks.com**

THE LATE WILLIAM A. FOSTER, Q.C.

From a painting by WM. CUTTS, Esq., the property of the National Club.

A Memorial

OF THE LATE

WILLIAM A. FOSTER, Q.C.

With Introduction

BY

GOLDWIN SMITH, D.C.L.

Toronto:

HUNTER, ROSE & COMPANY.

1890.

PREFATORY NOTE.

SHORTLY after the death of William A. Foster, the design was entertained of issuing, as a memorial of him, one or two of his literary productions for distribution among a few friends, together with some extracts from the obituary notices which had appeared in the Canadian Press. Mr. Foster's writings were on a variety of topics, though dealing chiefly with the national movement, known as "Canada First," of which, it may be said, he was himself a part. In 1875, when the movement, from various causes, began to wane, Mr. Foster devoted himself almost exclusively to his profession and wrote hardly anything for publication. Since then, some of those associated with him in the Canada First organization desired that its literature should be gathered and published; and, after his death, the expression of this desire was renewed, coupled with the wish to have some memorial of him whom they had known and loved, and who had been so largely identified with the patriotic movement. In response to these requests, the little volume which now appears has been published. In departing from the original. design, of issuing a volume only for a limited circle of private readers, the apology must be the importunity of friends. But the issue of the volume may not be amiss if it tends to keep green the memory of one who was not unworthy the regard and affection bestowed upon him, and if it serve to perpetuate the feeling which inspired "Canada First," namely, ardent patriotism and loyal devotion to the highest interests of the country.

The opportunity is here taken of recording a grateful sense of the kindness of many friends, who have shown an interest in the work and furthered its publication. Among those to whom the writer is specially indebted are Professor Goldwin Smith, Mr. Henry J. Morgan, and Mr. G. Mercer Adam.

To. Mr. Goldwin Smith a special debt is due, for readily complying with the request to enrich the volume with an introduction. His characteristic kindness is greatly appreciated. An honoured friend of Mr. Foster, he has given to the publication a value which the reader will, doubtless, highly esteem.

To the Directors of the National Club, and to Mr. Wm. Cutts, of the Ontario Society of Artists, hearty thanks are tendered for permission to reproduce in this volume the very excellent portrait painted by Mr. Cutts for the Club.

M. B. F.

TORONTO, Oct., 1890.

INTRODUCTION.

THE long train of mourners which on the 3rd of November, 1888, attended the body of William Alexander Foster to the tomb, was following not only the funeral of a man of bright intellect, high professional promise, winning character, and many friends, but of one who had represented an idea and been the animating spirit of a movement. The idea, for the time at least, died with him : the movement, if it did not end its march, halted at his grave. It must be owned that even before his death the light of the idea had been growing pale and the pace of the movement had become slow.

The union of the North American Colonies by Confederation, the appeals of the authors of Confederation to the patriotism and self-reliance of the people, the glorious pictures which were then drawn of the greatness and resources of the country, could not fail to awaken strong emotions and kindle high hopes in the breasts of Canadians, especially in those of the young. It happened also that just then a generation of native Canadians, or men who had immigrated in childhood, were growing up to manhood and aspired to fill the high places of public life, of the professions, and of commerce, theretofore held

by men from the Old Country, who were at this time passing off the scene. The withdrawal of British troops
had also helped to bring socially to the front young natives who had been thrown into the background by the
social ascendancy of the British officer. W. A. Foster
had graduated in law at Toronto University, had studied
in the office of Mr. (now Sir Adam,) Wilson, and had written for the press, not only political and commercial, but
comic, for he had a kindly vein of humour. He had a
share, with Mr. Hugh Scott, in founding our great commercial paper, *The Monetary Times*. Mr. Charles Lindsey,
than whom there could be no better judge, thought very
highly of his promise as a journalist. One of his com-
rades in journalism, was Adam Clarke Tyner, his obituary
article on whom is here reprinted. The fire of national
aspiration and patriotism burned in Foster. In 1866
he sent two papers on Confederation to the *Westminster
Review*. In the same year he paid a visit to England,
where, thanks to the friendship of Mr. W. F. Rae, the
writer, he conversed with Mr. Robert Lowe (now Lord
Sherbrooke), George Eliot, and the poet Browning. In
1871 he produced the memorable pamphlet "Canada
First," which leads the series of his productions in this
volume. Some things in that pamphlet, when we now
read it in cold blood, may seem to belong to the heyday
of Confederation and of youth. But its effect at the time
was great. It embodied a prevailing sentiment, gave
shape to a floating idea, and called into existence the
group of sympathizing spirits known by the collective

name of " Canada First." The aim of Canada First was never very clearly defined. Some of the group, borne on by the tide of the time, aspired more or less consciously, more or less openly, to an independent nationality. Others aspired to a nationality which they deemed possible without independence, and desired only to complete the measure of Canadian self-government, make the interest of Canada paramount in our policy, and fill all offices with men who, whether natives or not, were thoroughly Canadian in spirit. Some, perhaps, as the programme presently to be quoted indicates, had partly in view commercial legislation on the line since designated as the National Policy. To some probably Canada First was rather a vague sentiment than a distinct opinion or idea. All however united in striving to cultivate Canadian patriotism, to raise Canada above the rank of a mere dependency, and to give her the first place in Canadian hearts.

To attempt to give anything like a list of " Canada First " men might be unsafe. The nominations for the Council and Officers of the Association, which in time became its centre (January 6th, 1874), were Messrs. W. H. Howland, W. A. Foster, Wm. Canniff, M.D , Hugh Scott, R. W. Elliott, J. M. Trout, Jos. E. Macdougall, Wm. Badenach, W. G. McWilliams, C. E. English, James Michie, G. M. Rae, Nicol Kingsmill, Hugh Blain, Jos. A. Donovan, W. B. McMurrich, J. K. Macdonald, T. C. Scoble, Richard Grahame, Fred. Fenton, G. W. Badgerow, C. W. R. Biggar, W. H. Fraser, J. G. Ridout, James R. Roaf, Thomas

Walmsley, W. E. Cornell, W. G. Mutton, C. W. Dedrickson, J. Crickmore, William Hessin, J. Ritchie, jr., R. G. Trotter, A. S. Irving, A. Howell, R. H. Gray, and A. M. Rosebrugh, M.D. In connection with these names should certainly be mentioned, as having more or less sympathized with the movement, Dr. Schultz, now Lieutenant-Governor of Manitoba, the late Chief Justice Moss, Dr. W. T. O'Reilly, late Inspector of Prisons and Asylums, Mr. Henry James Morgan, of the Secretary of State Department, Mr. Robert Grant Haliburton, the scientist and man of letters, Mr. George R. Kingsmill, journalist, Mr. Charles Mair, the poet, Mr. James H. Morris, Q.C., Mr. Frank McKelcan, Q.C., Mr. James H. Coyne, and Mr. William Norris. Perhaps the most prominent figure of the group, Foster's temperament leading him usually to remain in the background, was that of Mr. W. H. Howland, who may be regarded as the chief founder both of the Canadian National Association and the National Club. But as to the whole number it must be repeated that they were not members of an organized party in politics with defined aims, but partakers in a general sentiment. We cannot pretend to state the extent to which each of them sympathised with the movement, or with any part or object of it, at the time, much less to state the extent to which they have retained such feelings since. The eyes of all Canada First men were turned with hope to Mr. Edward Blake, a native Canadian, whose star was then rising in all its brightness above the political horizon, and after Mr. Blake to Mr. Thomas Moss, who having graduated with brilliant honours at Toronto University, was rapidly mounting to eminence at the Bar. The circle greatly cherished the memory of the martyred Thomas D'Arcy McGee, as that of a Canadian patriot who had conceived high hopes for the country, and given them eloquent expression.*

Canada First did not ally itself to either of the political parties. Its avowed aim was to put the country above them both, as Foster's article, "Party *versus* Principles," included among these remains, will show. When, in the autumn of 1873, Mr. Moss became a candidate for the representation of West Toronto in the Dominion Parliament, as he had the nomination of the Liberal party, Canada First could not join his organization, but as he was its man it gave him a hearty support and held a meeting in his favour. "In the outlying Provinces," said Foster at that meeting, "old party lines have been destroyed and they care nothing for the questions which have divided us in the older Provinces, but if the Canadian National party can give them a national sentiment, there will then be something of a bond of union between them and us in the future." He repudiated nativism, saying that what we wanted was that every immigrant should become a Canadian as on the other

* It is right to say with regard to this and the preceding paragraph, that the writer of this notice had not settled in Canada when the movement commenced or when "Canada First" was published. Nor was he in the country when the Canadian National Association was formed or when *The Nation* newspaper was brought out. He therefore speaks, in part at least, not from personal knowledge, but from the best information which he can obtain.

side of the line every immigrant became an American. He concluded by moving: "That it is the duty of all Canadians, whether such by birth or adoption to recognize the pressing necessity for the cultivation of a national sentiment which will unite the people of the various Provinces more closely in the bonds of citizenship, promote a mutual confidence whose common source of affection will prompt acts of toleration and bonds of respect, and prove the best safeguard of our Dominion against absorption on the one hand or disunion on the other. That an organization which will draw the line between Canadians loyal to their soil and those who place their citizenship in a subordinate or secondary position, affords the surest means of cementing a confederation and securing political action in the interests of the whole Dominion." The Conservative Press called the meeting a Grit intrigue, and denounced all who were connected with it. Mr. Moss was triumphantly elected, and the hopes of Canada First rose.

In October, 1874, Mr. Edward Blake made his famous Aurora speech which, somewhat enigmatic though it was, all the world interpreted as the proclamation of a new departure in the direction of Independence. That we were "four millions of Britons who were not free" was the keynote of this memorable deliverance, and those words were everywhere repeated though with widely different emotions. By Canada First the speech was hailed with delight. By the old leaders of the Liberal party, whose Liberalism had ended with the attainment of responsible government, it was received with consternation and disgust, as an alarming outbreak of free thought in the party camp. Their journal suspended the report of the speech, while an editorial was being prepared to neutralize its evil effect, and from that day never ceased to denounce Canada First and to shoot arrows which were well understood to be intended for Mr. Blake, though they might be ostensibly levelled against some safer target. Mr. Blake, however, pursued his course, and under his auspices *The Liberal* was set up at Toronto as an independent rival of *The Globe.* Both the old political parties frowned on Canada First, though it was only the natural response to the appeals made by their leaders to Canadian patriotism for the purpose of carrying Confederation. But the Old School Liberals, or to use their familiar name, the Grits, and their organ were always its bitterest enemies. It was their camp which it chiefly menaced with mutiny, and their party strategy which it most threatened to mar. This will explain some passages in Foster's addresses.

In the same year (1874), the Canadian National Association, comprising those who took the more active part in the movement, was formed. The list of its prominent members has already been given. It issued an address to the people of Canada, which will be found among the papers of this volume. The address is signed by Mr. Wm. H. Howland, as Chairman, and Mr. W. G. McWilliams, as Secretary ; but it is believed Foster had a large share in its composition. It is headed " Canada First." It vindicates the movement against the interpretations of those who identify it with Annexation, Independence, or Know-nothingism, and explains that the aim is broad patriotism, with national unity and a full measure of self-government. It denounces the narrow spirit of party and the prostration of independent thought beneath the chariot-wheels of mere dictators, that is, the dictator of *The Globe.*

At a dinner given by the Hamilton Branch to the Toronto Branch, Foster made a speech, the keynote of which was that "the time had arrived for Canadians to say that they had a country, and that the bearing of the sentimental upon the actual might be more important than was supposed." He went over at the same time the several planks in the Canadian National Association Platform :—

1. British Connection, Consolidation of the Empire—and in the meantime a voice in treaties affecting Canada.
2. Closer trade relations with the British West India Islands, with a view to ultimate political connection.
3. Income Franchise.
4. The Ballot, with the addition of compulsory voting.
5. A Scheme for the Representation of Minorities.
6. Encouragement of Immigration, and Free Homesteads in the Public Domain.
7. The imposition of duties for Revenue, so adjusted as to afford every possible encouragement to Native Industry.
8. An Improved Militia System, under command of trained Dominion Officers.

9. No Property Qualifications in Members of the House of Commons.

10. The Reorganization of the Senate.

11. Pure and Economic Administration of Public Affairs.

It was before the Canadian National Association that Foster delivered, in 1875, the address here reprinted. In that address he went beyond the first article of the platform and avowed, though without breach of constitutional loyalty, the real aspirations of the more pronounced and ardent members of the circle. " We no more advocate Independence than we advocate the Day of Judgment. There are those among us who think just as Mr. Gladstone, Mr. Lowe, Mr. Brown, Sir Alexander Galt, Mr. Blake and others, think, that the relations of Canada to the Empire are proper subjects for discussion ; that some day or other separation may or must come, and that now is the time at least to begin to prepare for it. England has been trying for years to make us stand upon our feet. The troops have been withdrawn. We are allowed to legislate as we please and there is great dislike of interfering with our action. It would rather take us aback if at some early day we were made to strike out for ourselves without any preparation for the event. What must come is either a Federation of the Empire or Independence." Such avowals of course drew volleys of vituperation from the regular party organs on both sides. " Canada First" was denounced as " annexationism," " Republicanism," " treason" and " Communism," the orthodox Liberal organ as usual leading the chorus.

"Canada First" was no more annexationist than it was Communist. Its leading idea was a nationality too strong in its unity to be absorbed by the United States. On the subject of the Fenian Raids and the questions connected with them, Foster, as a journalist, had written in an ardently patriotic strain. He wrote in an equally ardent strain about Riel's first rebellion in the North-West and the murder of Thomas Scott.

The Nation, a weekly journal, was brought out in 1874, by a group of Canada First men, among whom Foster probably was the most active. Mr. W. H. Howand also took a leading part. Mr. Charles Lindsey lent the young journal from the first the powerful aid of his pen. So did Mr. W. J. Rattray, one of our best and most thoughtful writers, and a great friend of Foster, who was destined to a too short career.* Its aim was, in accordance with the title, to be thoroughly national and independent of party, and of all interests opposed to the broadest patriotism. It also sought to give the country a literary paper, and one which should treat general questions in a more comprehensive way and more satisfactorily than they could be treated by the party press. *The Nation* ran for two years, and considering the limited character of the constituency to which such a journal could appeal in a country like ours, with success. Its circulation was larger in proportion to the area than that of its prototype in the United States. At the end of two years, its two principal writers were

---

* The writer of this notice contributed, but at a later stage.

obliged to leave it ; they could not be replaced and *The
Nation* was withdrawn. A constant fire had been kept
up against it by enemies, who in their eagerness to destroy it and crush its contributors, broke through the
laws of Press warfare ; but few, it is believed, thought
that by its character and tone, it had disgraced Canada
First.

The National Club, founded at Toronto in 1874, was
another offspring of the movement in which Foster took
an active interest. Its name was an antithesis to those of
party clubs, and it was destined to unite under the same
roof all true Canadians and to afford them a place for
perfectly free intercourse and discussion, in a social way,
about the concerns and interests of their common
country.

In 1875, however, the movement received a heavy blow.
The man to whom it looked as its leader, Mr. Edward
Blake, joined the Liberal Ministry, the head of which was
Mr. Alexander Mackenzie, but the real master of which
was Mr. George Brown, the proprietor of *The Globe*, the
bitterest enemy of " Canada First." *The Liberal* was at
the same time withdrawn. From the consequences of
this catastrophe the central action of the movement did
not recover, though the sentiment survived elsewhere.
Mr. Moss soon afterwards quitted Parliament for the
Bench, of which he had become one of the greatest orna-
ments when he was snatched away by a too early death.
Foster devoted himself to his profession. He had made
for himself a happy home, by his marriage in 1877 with

Margaret, the daughter of Ex-Mayor Bowes. He was rising rapidly at the Bar and had been made a Q.C., when overwork, in connection with the Central Bank Liquidation, broke down his health and hurried him to the grave. In years his life was short; in interest and significance it was long.

His bright and winning expression has been well preserved in the portrait of him by Mr. W. Cutts, a wonderful work considering that it was executed from a photograph after the death of the subject.

High aspiration followed by disinterested effort works into and elevates the character of a nation as it works into and elevates the character of a man. That is the epitaph which must be written on the tomb of many a generous movement. That is the epitaph which, if there is no revival in store, will be written on the tomb of Canada First.

A Voyage down the St. Lawrence in a Raft, which concludes the series, shows Foster's literary gifts as well as the geniality and mirthfulness, which made his company always a delight and his departure a heavy loss to a large circle of friends.

G. S.

CANADA FIRST.*

————o————

THREE hundred and thirty-seven years ago Jacques Cartier erected the cross at Gaspé, and, amid the triumphal shout of his hardy mariners, flung to the breeze the *Fleur-de-lis* of Old France. Since then what a land of adventure and romance has this been! We may have no native ballad for the nursery, or home-born epic for the study; no tourney feats to rhapsodise over, or mock heroics to emblazon on our escutcheon; we may have no prismatic fables to illumine and adorn the preface of our existence, or curious myths to obscure and soften the sharp outline of our early history; yet woven into the tapestry of our past, are whole volumes of touching poetry and great tomes of glowing prose that rival fiction in eagerness of incident, and in marvellous climax put fable to the blush. We need not ransack foreign romance for valorous deeds, nor are we compelled to go abroad for sad tales of privation and suffering. The most chivalrous we can match; the most tried we can parallel. Each stage of this country's progress recounts to us, in all the simplicity of unpremeditated record, sacrifices endured, hardships encountered and brave deeds done, not amid the applause of an interested and anxious world, nor yet amid the pomp

*Reprinted from a *brochure*, published at Toronto in the year 1871, entitled "Canada First; or, Our New Nationality." An Address by W. A. Foster, Esq., *Barrister at Law*.

and pride of oft-recurring circumstance, but rather in
silent, ever-changing strait and myriad-formed danger,
when every faculty sprang into earnest, vigorous action,
and every sense grew sharp by reason of restless emer-
gency; when civilization grappled with herculean sav-
agery, and man fought with nature; and when, alas! the
consciousness of duty done was the sole reward achieved,
or the solitary unnamed mound, chapleted by the winter's
snow, was the only monument won. Yet there are few
heroes in our Pantheon. Where every man does his
duty, heroes are not wanted and are not missed.

For years our frontier echoed to the roar of battle;
the shrill scream of the Indian and the hoarse yell of the
white man mingling in death agony; while along the
dim corridors of our forests the unpitying north wind
came laden with the half-stifled sighs of lonely, yet
patient women, and the shivering wail of starving children. In the old times war raged almost continuously,
and every man was a soldier. First came the contests with
the Iroquois and the Hurons, garnished with sad tales of
civilized atrocities and savage vengeance. If one's appetite for horrors demands gratification, the needful
stimulant may be found in the details of the Massacre
of Lachine, when 1,400 Iroquois warriors swooped down
by night upon a slumbering village, and plied the torch
and tomahawk with all the relentlessness of savage hate,
showing mercy to neither age nor sex, and reserving
only for a sickening butchery those whom the inexorable
flame spared. Two hundred men, women and children
were burnt alive, and those who died under prolonged
tortures were not a few. Houses, crops, everything was

reduced to ashes, and woe held exultant sway amid deso-
lation and blood. Next came the wars between England
and France, with their mimic reproduction on this continent; the ambitions, animosities and jealousies of European diplomacy bringing devastation and death into
Canadian homes; and the swaying incidents of the Old
World finding their obsequious parallel, three thousand
miles across the sea, in the wilds of the New. In vain
the New Englander made desperate and persistent efforts
to win Canada. In spite of repeated invasions, and in
the face of large odds, the flag of France kept proudly
afloat. A people varying in number from 25,000 in 1679,
to 70,000 in 1761, not only thwarted every attempt at
their subjugation by the much more densely populated
colonies to the south, but with a little stingily rendered
assistance from the parent country, held their own against
repeated attack by land and sea. Mournful is the history
of those days. There were no ambulance trains then, no
Christian charities to assuage the horrors of battle, and
little skill to alleviate its sufferings. Mercy was a word
unknown, for the civilized had become apt pupils of the
savage. Need I rehearse in your ears the terrible punishment inflicted on the simple-minded, inoffensive Acadians
who "dwelt in the love of God and of man,"—"their
dwellings open as day and the hearts of the owners,"—
when hundreds of families were torn apart, wife from
husband, child from parent, and

> "the freighted vessels departed,
> Bearing a nation, with all its household gods, into exile,
> Exile without an end, and without an example in story;"

discharging their living cargoes at intervals along the
coast from Boston to Carolina, and flinging like outcasts

among a people alien in race and language, those home-
less, houseless, broken-hearted wanderers. O! it was a
cruel act without palliation, an inhuman vengeance without excuse! *   Who has not read of Evangeline, her heart
filled with inexpressible sweetness, pursuing through the
slow-revolving years the phantom of her love, and losing
the celestial brightness of her girlhood in " the unsatis-
fied longing, and the dull, deep pain and constant anguish
of patience;" or of Gabriel, " weary with waiting, un-
happy and restless, seeking in the western wilds, oblivion
of self and of sorrow ;" or of the dying Marguerite, of
whom the sweet-voiced Whittier has sung:

"Done was the work of her hands, she had eaten her bitter bread ;
The world of the alien people lay behind her, dim and dead,
But her soul went back to its child-time; she saw the sun o'erflow
With gold the Basin of Minas, and set over Gaspereau ;
She saw the face of her mother, she heard the song she sang,
And far off, faintly, slowly, the bell for vespers rang."

But pathetic incident must give place before the march
of historical event.   It was not until wearied out by incessant attack, deserted by parent land, and overborne
by superior numbers, that the French-Canadian laid
down his arms and exchanged his allegiance.   In the
spring of 1758, 30,000 British combatants were ready to
march on Canada, not merely raw militiamen, but regular troops as well, led by officers trained on European
battle-fields, armed with artillery and siege requisites,
and supported by an active and daring fleet.   The Canadians knew their danger and prepared to meet it.   An
inquest of the inhabitants was held, and the male popu-

* Foster had not read Parkman, Adams, Archibald, and Kingsford.

lation of the colony between the ages of sixteen and sixty
was found to be but 15,000. Aid was implored from
France, but instead of munitions of war and recruits, the
devoted colonists were vouchsafed official despatches
recommending them to dispute every inch of territory,
foot to foot with the British and to sustain the honour of
the French arms to the utmost. " Not only would additional troops be a means of aggravating the evils of the
dearth which has too long afflicted the colony,"—wrote
the French Minister—" but the chances are great that if
sent thither, they would be captured on their way to you
by the British." Though thus basely deserted; though
exhausted by continual marching and incessant fighting;
though their dwellings were falling to ruin and their
fields lay waste; though their wives and children were
crying for bread ; the despised and forsaken French-Can-
adians neither flung aside their allegiance nor forgot their
honour, but plunged into the final struggle with a devotion which excites our wonder and admiration. It was
of no avail. On the 13th September, 1759, Quebec was
taken. One year afterwards the French flag was hauled
down and Canada became part of the British Empire.
Great was the joy manifested in England over the con-
quest of Louis XIV's "acres of snow." Addresses were
presented to the king, congratulating him on this much-
coveted addition to the Imperial possessions ; a statue
in Westminster Abbey was accorded to Wolfe; public
thanks were decreed to each of the chief officers who had
taken part in the Quebec expedition ; and it was ordered
that prayers of thanksgiving should be offered up to
Heaven throughout the whole empire.

B

But change of rulers did not bring permanent peace to the harassed colonists. Sixteen years after Wolfe took Quebec, Canada again became the scene of war. The American Revolution broke out, and Canada, with a population of about 70,000 was called upon to meet the attack of a people numbering 3,000,000. Every art of persuasion was tried in vain by the Revolutionists to win the Canadians to their side ; due provision was made in the Federal Constitution for the admission of Canada into the new confederacy, but without the anticipated result. Then it was concluded that more severe measures should be resorted to, in order to bring the refractory and blind inhabitants of this ice-clad region to a proper sense of their interests, if not their duty. One enthusiastic American Colonel proposed to conquer and hold the whole country with 2,000 men. Finally, Canada was invaded by an army under General Schuyler, but, after a futile effort to carry out his instructions to take Quebec, Montreal, and other places, the General withdrew.

At the close of the Revolutionary War, twenty-five thousand persons, exiles from the States, sought refuge in Canada. When we call to mind that there was not a tree cut from Ottawa to Kingston, a distance of 150 miles, that Kingston was a village of a few huts, and that around the shores of Lakes Ontario and Erie all was a dense wilderness, we can form some idea of the hardships that fell to the lot of those who sacrificed everything but honour, on the shrine of allegiance. Remember that the fighting done during the revolutionary war was not monopolized by the regular troops of Great Britain ; there were corps and regiments of American loyalists with familiar titles and designations. They had their King's Rangers and Queen's Rangers, the Prince of Wales' American Volunteers, Georgia Loyalists, New Jersey Volunteers, Loyal New Englanders, Maryland Loyalists, Pennsylvania Loyalists, and so on, just as we have our Queen's Own or the Prince of Wales' regiment. Yet, when peace was made between Britain and the States, those loyalists who had placed their lives and property in peril were left to the tender mercies of the revolutionists, without any stipulation as to their protection, without any security even for their lives. Lord Loughborough spoke truly when in his place in the House of Lords he said : "In ancient or modern history there has not been so shameful a desertion of men who have sacrificed all to their duty, and to their reliance upon British faith." Lord North spoke in like terms : "Never were the honour, the principles, the policy of a nation so grossly abused as in the desertion of those men, who are now exposed to every punishment that vengeance and poverty can inflict because they were not rebels." Exile was the reward of those who had been forsaken by king and country, and thus Canada became the home of those whom we call the U.E. Loyalists.

Thirty years after the acknowledgment of American Independence came the war of 1812, with Canada once more the battle-ground. An Act was passed by Congress calling 100,000 volunteers into active service, but the Canadians were neither deceived by proclamations nor dismayed by threats. A call to arms rang throughout the country, echoing from lake to river, and piercing the inmost recesses of the forest. How the eyes of the

old refugee loyalists must have flashed as the rusty flint-
lock was taken from the rack above the fire-place, and
the recollection of by-gone hardships and persecution
came surging up from the past! How must the pulses of
the young men have throbbed as they grasped the trusty
rifle, and, amid the sudden silence of home preparation
for departure, pondered over the sad story of their parents'
exile. Now there was opportunity for redressing old
wrongs that clung to memory with fierce tenacity!
There was no calculation of the chances of success; no
reckoning over the probable consequences of failure.
All that they had forgotten was their desertion, in the
hour of peril, by king and country. There were but
280,000 people all told in Upper and Lower Canada, yet
the event justified their self-confidence. General Hull
with 2,500 men invaded Canada by way of Sandwich,
and then surrendered himself and his army prisoners of
war at Detroit. General Van Rensellaer appeared at
Queenston with 2,000 men, but only to surrender at
least 900 of them. General Smyth landed 3,000 men at
Fort Erie, but was at once driven back. General Pike
brought 2,500 men as far as Little York, where he and
200 of them were blown into the air by an explosion at
the Old Fort. General Winchester led 1,000 men to
Frenchtown, near Detroit, but their end was capture.
General Dearborne, with 3,000 men, was defeated at
Stony Creek. General Harrison, with 2,500 men, was
beaten at Fort Meigs. General Wilkinson, with 3,000
men, was utterly routed at Chrysler's Farm. General
Hampden set out with a grand army of 8,000 men to capture Montreal, but he suffered an ignominious defeat from

a handful of Canadian militia under De Salaberry.
General McClure succeeded in taking Niagara, but
Hampden's defeat caused him to retire. General Brown
crossed at Black Creek with 5,000 men, but after the experience at Lundy's Lane and Fort Erie, deemed it
prudent to withdraw. At no point along the frontier did
the invaders gain any important advantage, and when
the war ended, Canada had not lost one inch of territory.

These are merely historical facts, but it is just as well
to keep them at our fingers' end, for they are not unpleasant to reflect upon. Were we disposed to vaunt ourselves, we might come down to more modern times, and
ask : Was there a display of timidity in the Trent affair?
Did Canadians hold back when the sanctity of our
common flag was violated ? Were reasons for neutrality
in the impending struggle searched out with eagerness ?
Or did our people sigh over their little hoards of money
—the fruit of years of hard work—or look with fainting
heart at the scarce-born evidences of substantial progress
that surrounded them ? Like the everlasting fire on the
altar, loyalty gave forth a steady light, its flame never
brighter or more pure than in the hour of national peril.
Think you, now, that Canada has no claim to rank with
those lands where adventure has had play and romance
has had a home, or that the heroic devotion which distinguished its inhabitants, of French and British origin,
is less worthy of a place in story than the most cherished
traditions of the Old World.

But our past is characterised by something more than
romantic attachment to a flag, or chivalrous devotion to

an idea. Sentiment did not blunt the edge of industry, nor suffering give excuse for idleness. Every breathing spell of war gave the husbandman opportunity. The sword and musket were exchanged for the plough and sickle; and a fruitful soil, feeling the warm glow of peace, yielded a grateful return. The forest echoed the ring of the axe and the crash of timber. Amid the solitariness of the backwoods the sturdy settler was hewing out a home for himself and his family, with hunger and cold kept merely at arm's length. Between him and his nearest neighbour, miles of dark forest intervened. The traveller or trader picked his way across tangled brush-wood and fallen timber, or tramped wearily over a trackless wilderness of snow, finding few finger-posts by the road-side to point out the direction he wished to take. All kinds of field-work were done by hand, for there were very few oxen and still fewer horses. In 1789, the mails left Upper Canada for England about twice a year, so that epistolary effort was not much taxed. For years the only road from Lower Canada was by the St. Lawrence, the rapids being ascended by canoes and bateaux in ten or twelve days, until the flat-bottomed Durham boats, steered with a ten-foot pole and pushed along by two men on each side, came into use. We can read in the *York Gazette*, of April 29th, 1815, that the Lieut.-Governor, Sir George Murray, Kt., arrived at York from Burlington, in a birch canoe. But none of us need go far to learn all about the hardships of the early settlers, for witnesses are still among us who passed through the ordeal. Now we can afford to look back with some degree of complacency, for industry has produced abun-

dant fruit, and we are reaping in joy a harvest sown in
tears and trouble. As farm after farm was rescued from
native wildness, schemes of internal improvement, first
viewed as shadowy impossibilities, grew into reality,
while the bounteous yield of a virgin soil sent new life
into every artery of trade. Land was gradually freed
from the tight-locking folds of rapacious hydras, and the
barnacles that fattened on the offices of state were torn
from the vitals of the country. What has been the
result? In 1812, the population of Canada was 280,000;
to-day Canada has over four millions of people. In 1806,
the value of the exports from the whole of the Provinces
was $928,000; last year our exports were over seventy-
three millions, and our imports over seventy-four millions
of dollars. In 1815, the first steamboat was built on
Lake Ontario; to-day Canada is the third maritime
power in the world, with *six* million tons entered in-
wards, and *five* million tons entered outwards, engaged in
carrying on our trade. In 1851, Canada had but fifty-
five miles of railway ; to-day there are three thousand
miles in operation, several hundreds of miles under construction, and a scheme on foot to build 2,500 miles more
that will present a route between England and Japan,
1,100 miles shorter than by New York and San Fran-
cisco, and give us a continuous line of four thousand
miles across the continent. We possess a system of canals
the most complete in the world, that cost us twenty
millions of dollars,—so complete indeed that President
Grant looks upon it as part of the St. Lawrence navigation. The aggregate of our banking capital is over thirty-six millions of dollars, and the savings of our people

represented by deposits in our monetary institutions, amount to about sixty-four millions.

We have coal in Nova Scotia, on the Atlantic; coal at the Saskatchewan, in the heart of the continent; and coal at Vancouver's Island, on the Pacific. We have mineral wealth as various as our needs, and, in extent, boundless. We have, at our doors, exhaustless fisheries, the richest in the world, furnishing an annual yield estimated at twenty million dollars to the various countries engaged in them, and giving us a nursery for adventurous and hardy seamen. Our agricultural product is immense, and capable of indefinite expansion; and our forests are the envy of the world. We have, or will have shortly, 70,000 sailors, and now have at least 700,000 men between the ages of 20 and 60 available for defensive purposes. As for territory, we have more than half the continent, and elbow-room for a population of 40,000,000. Religious freedom exists here in its most perfect form, and our elaborate system of common schools, colleges and universities gives an equal opportunity to all to achieve distinction. We have political institutions combining the greatest freedom with the most perfect restraint upon riot, recognizing the rights of the people without begetting distrust or disrespect for lawful authority: neither ignoring the poor nor bringing terror to the rich; giving voice to property without drowning the tones of labour; allowing complete self-government by means of a graduated jurisdiction and, through a well-understood and easily-enforced system of responsibility, admitting of reform without revolution, government without despotism. Our Dominion Legislature will compare favourably with any deliberative body in the world. Accident may have brought to the surface of politics a good many who float by reason of the cork-like lightness of their brains ; but, on the whole, our public men are as able as those of other countries. Our politicians have certainly carried party strife to the extreme, but it is an axiom that the smaller the pit, the more fiercely do the rats fight. The world would be rather a stupid place if all men thought and acted alike. The charms of novelty and variety are too attractive, even to the idlest and most listless, to render an unbroken harmony either pleasant to the eye or grateful to the ear. Diversities of temper, of understanding, of interest, are necessary to stimulate our love of existence; our impulses, offensive and defensive, serving as a preservative from mental paralysis, as a preventive as regards public langour and impotence, and as a safeguard against the enervating influences of a dreary, monotonous dulness. The old Norse mythology, with its Thor hammers and Thor hammerings, appeals to us,—for we are a Northern people,— as the true out-crop of human nature, more manly, more real, than the weak marrow-bones superstition of an effeminate South. For the purposes of attrition, the bigoted dotard, the reckless empiric, and the shallow babbler are useful in their way, as are also the wise, the cautious, and the prudent. To produce the fine flour, we must have a nether as well as an upper mill-stone. We cannot construct politicians, nor manufacture political parties impromptu, for there is always an inert mass, incapable of sudden emotion, subject merely to that oscillation which gives victory or defeat. One might as well try to form a political party from persons of a peculiar physiognomy, as to fit men into sets of political principles. They must come together naturally or not at all, for men cannot be sized in principles, as if at company drill. Let the worst come, however; we know that political parties have their beginning and their end. Babels are built and confusion of tongues ensues. But when discussion is pushed to the extreme, and enthusiasts and demagogues have gone mad, the turning-point is reached, and an union of those who have their senses left, marks the beginning of a new era. When the time does come for a renewal of strife, we spin around, in accordance with the immutable laws by which the political world is regulated, and we cannot, if we would, avoid the scrambling, jostling, quarrelling and fighting, incident to the enjoyment of free institutions in a free country. However, if there be a common object in view, and that the welfare of the country, it is best for us not to complain too much.

Formerly, the Provinces, whose destinies are now linked, were disunited, knowing little, and caring less, about each other. Instead of an interchange of commodities, and of floating population, the current ran in a foreign direction, and thousands of our young men were not only lost to us, but went to the building up of our rivals— yes rivals! else what means this shutting us out with higher tariffs, thwarting us by harsh legislation, abrogating reciprocity treaties, and obstructing our development? But we were not always considered rivals. At one time the prospect looked gloomy enough. Old Canada was a dependency, with its best portion shut in from the seaboard for five months of the year; separated from those of kindred sympathies, and acknowledging a like allegiance, by an almost untraversable tract of country ; gazing at the prosperity of a nation that held out every inducement to unite with it ; without manufactures or capital, yet witnessing a stream of British wealth pouring into the lap of its overshadowing neighbour; thinly populated and outbid in attracting immigration. Times have changed, however, and there is no reason why this era should not be but the dawn of our prosperity. All that has been done here has been accomplished in the teeth of competition with a nation which calls itself, and is generally accepted as, the most enterprising of all nations ; which " beats all creation " in everything it does, " steals the keys from snoring Destiny," and outruns time in its hurry to do it. We have been alternately flattered and threatened, yet neither wile nor threat has mortgaged our country with dishonour, or caused us to sacrifice our identity. So if we take pride in the past there is some excuse for us ; if we hope for the future, we have, at least, some justification. Thanks to Dr. Ryerson, our school children have now the means of acquiring a knowledge of Canadian geography without first searching through every State in the American Union to find the country they live in, and can now learn something of Canadian history without first pumping dry the reservoir of Yankee buncombe.

Thus far, my object has been to indicate our advancement as a country and as a people, but it may be well to consider whether individual effort has kept pace, in individual results, with combined action and joint progress; whether the unit has distinguished itself when

isolated from the mass; whether the mind has grown
inert by reason of the need to supply mere bodily wants;
whether chopping and digging have blunted sensibilities,
and kept in the background the more refined ambitions
of the soul; whether our soil is more fertile than our
brains; whether scholarship and talent find in Canada a
congenial home.   It may be bold for mere colonists, mere
backwoodsmen, to venture on dangerous comparisons;
but let us hazard results.   There are Canadian names
known to the world, outside our boundaries, on which
renown has fallen, and we are entitled, at least, to claim
whatever credit is our due.   Thanks to the industry of
Mr. Morgan, we have not far to go for information.   Sir
William Logan is one of the great geologists of the day;
Sir Duncan Gibb is among the foremost in medical
science.   In Art, distinction has been attained by Canadians, one of whom flourished in Russia; Gilbert S.
Newton became famous for colour, and was made a
Royal Academican in London; Falardeau, a poor Quebec
boy, won celebrity in Italy.   Among ourselves there are
names we delight to honour—Paul Kane, Plamondon,
Bourassa, Berthon, Hamel, and Legare—all gifted artists.
We claim Sir Samuel Cunard, the father of steam
navigation on the Atlantic; Sir Hugh Allan, the largest
ship-owner in the world; and Sir Edward Belcher, the
first surveying officer of the day.   Scholarship and profound thought have not suffered from our practical
life.   Archaeological lore finds a master-spirit in Dr.
McCaul, of our national University, who is pronounced
by the *Saturday Review* to be a better scholar than any
of the antiquaries who have taken to the elucidation of

Britanno-Roman inscriptions. Dr. Wilson not only casts new light upon the archæology and pre-historic annals of Scotland, but dives into the ethnology and antiquities of America, with a zeal and success which evoke the admiration of those skilled in such subjects. From the Ottawa region, Mr. Todd sends forth the most useful and complete text-book that has ever appeared, on the practical operation of the British Constitution. John Foster Kirk, of New Brunswick, has, according to the highest critics, entitled himself to take rank with those accomplished historians, Prescott and Motley, by the production of his history of Charles the Bold. We can boast, too, of humourists, novelists, and tale-writers, who have distinguished themselves. Judge Haliburton, of Nova Scotia, has won fame through the sayings and doings of Sam Slick. Besides him, we claim Major Richardson, the author of " Wacousta ;" Professor de Mille, of New Brunswick, who wrote " The Dodge Family ;" Mr. Jenkins, the author of " Ginx's Baby ;" De Boucherville, Bourassa, and Lajoie, who have, in their writings, evidenced all the sparkle and dash of the true Frenchman ; Mrs. Fleming, of New Brunswick, known to American literature as Cousin May Carleton ; Rossana Leprohen ; Louisa Murray, who contributes to *Once a Week ;* and Mrs. Moodie, who has given us a vivid picture of old-time hardships, in her " Roughing it in the Bush." Our historians are Garneau, Christie, Murdock, MacMullen, Lindsey, and Canniff. In Charles Heavysege, the author of " Saul," and " Jepthah's Daughter," we have a dramatic poet of great imagination and feeling, whose productions were received with considerable wonder by foreign critics. One of the great Quarterlies, the *North British*, said : " This work is undoubtedly one of the most remarkable written out of Great Britain." " This copy," the critic goes on to remark, " was given to the writer of the present article by Mr. Nathaniel Hawthorne, to whose recommendation of this, to him and to us, unknown Canadian poet, our readers, and English literature generally, are beholden for their first introduction to a most curious work." Charles Sangster chants, in no unworthy strains, the beauties and sublimities of our great waters. Of him Dr. O. W. Holmes wrote, " His verse adds new interest to the woods and streams amidst which he sings, and embellishes the charms of the maidens he celebrates." The soul-stirring lyrics of Alexander McLachlan combine manly thought with apt and terse expression ; and those of us who have been fortunate enough to have familiarized ourselves with them, need not a Sir Archibald Alison to tell us that the author is one truly inspired with the genius of poetry. Isidore Ascher has sung tenderly and sweetly of household gods, in his " Voices from the Hearth ;" and Charles Mair, the Canadian Keats, tempts us with delicious melody away to the sunny hills of his own "Dreamland." *   However, we do not make pretence to having achieved, as a people, great renown in literature.   " The Family Physician," and " Every Man his own Lawyer," are still purchased with avidity, while the poem or the essay lies on the bookseller's shelf, accumulating dust and respectability ; though, in this

---

* Those who desire to acquaint themselves with the best efforts of our song writers will find the Rev. E. H. Dewart's collection very useful.

particular, we are perhaps no worse off than our neighbours. We have done well, everything considered, and
our cousins across the lines have little room to brag over
us, as there are not a dozen names in their literature
that can be placed in the front rank among the poets,
historians, and novelists of to-day.

In the annals of war, Canadians have achieved distinction for skill and valour. The old French times give
to us the names of D'Iberville, of Montreal, who was re-
puted the most skilful naval officer in the service of
France, and of DeLéry, of Quebec, one of its first military
engineers. Need we call the roll of those Canadians who
have done battle for Britain? Major-General Dunn
campaigned in Egypt, Italy and Spain; Major-General
Beckwith fought at the Nile and at Waterloo; Admiral
Sir Provo Wallis captured the Chesapeake; Admiral
Watt figured in a hundred engagements; Admiral Sir
George Westphal was wounded on board the *Victory* at
Trafalgar; Sir Thos. Wiltshire served in India and in the
Peninsular war; Captain McNab of Toronto, was on
Picton's staff at Waterloo; Sir Richard England led the
3rd division at Inkerman; Sir Fenwick Williams won
fame at Kars, and Sir John Inglis at Lucknow; Col.
Dunn, of Toronto, was selected, as the bravest of the immortal Six Hundred, to receive the Victoria Cross; Read
of Perth, though a surgeon, won the same reward of valour for daring feats in the Indian mutiny. Side by side
with the soldier of the motherland, the Canadian fought
with equal devotion, and fell with equal honour. The
hot sun of India looks down upon the graves of Monti-
zambert, Evans, Joly, Sewell, and Vaughan; in the

Crimea Parker fell with his face to the foe; and on the ramparts of the Redan died Welsford, with the bloom of youth glowing on his cheek, and all a boy's enthusiasm fresh at his heart.

We have still another record of competition and success which is worthy of reference. The great British Universities have not been left untried by Canadians. Hincks, of Toronto, Redpath, of Montreal, Vidal, of Sarnia, proved that it is possible for our young men to compete successfully with the best. At the Staff College, at Sandhurst, Ridout, of Toronto, headed the list of candidates from all branches of the service. Robinson, of Toronto, came out fourth, and Benson, of St. Catharines, was the recipient of special honours for the high stand he took. Even the great Public Schools of England have not been essayed in vain. Not long ago Plumb, of Niagara, was the head boy at Rugby.

But with so much reason for self-felicitation, we are not apprehensive that vanity will obtain undue ascendency in the national character—for some time at least. Lest we should feel disposed to vaunt ourselves unduly, it may be well to bear in mind that Canada has been frequently spoken of with contempt. The normal Old-World idea respecting us and our country resolves itself into huge pictures, in which frost and snow, falling timber, snow shoes, furs, and wild Indians are the most prominent, if not the only, objects of vision. Peculiar notions are suggested by the word "Colony," so that it requires no great dexterity in intonation to use it as an efficient term of reproach. We know that when the absence of a criminal was desired, he was transported to a colony; when a political or religious zealot became obnoxious, he fled or was banished to a colony; when a ne'er-do-weel" was to be got rid of, he was assisted to a colony. Wild spirits sought it through love of adventure; persons of strong religious convictions braved its unknown dangers through enthusiasm; and, when resources grew narrow and bread scarce, gnawing poverty drove into the emigrant-ship many a true man and noble woman, snapping heart-strings that would not be untied, uprooting tender associations that seemed incapable of disentanglement, and unveiling to the rude gaze of the stranger all those sanctities of emotion whose shrine is the innermost tabernacle of our being. The tremulous farewells wafted from the ship's side, were but the prelude to a new life of heroic purpose and resolute action. We can scarcely wonder, therefore, that the word 'colony' carries with it some awkward as well as sad significations. The establishment of the colonies of Ancient Greece was occasioned by necessity; those of Rome by utility; and those of modern Europe by greed and ambition. The American Colonies were looked upon as feeders to the Mother Land, their resources being regarded as so much plunder for home enterprise, and their population as legitimate prey for home avarice. In the old French times Canada was farmed out to monopolists; and even when French Canadians here were fighting for their very existence against large odds, Frenchmen in France were writing disparagingly of them, as "a people who multiplied slowly in the woods, who associated with savages, but who furnished no return to the royal exchequer, no soldier to the royal host, no colonial merchandise to the

C

home trader." Brave Canadian officers were slighted and displaced to make room for the indigent yet supercilious favourites of the home authorities; and we read that the appointment of the Marquis de Vaudreuil, as governor of Montreal, was conceded with much hesitation, because his countess was a native Canadian. Coming down to more modern times, we can appease our hunger for criticism and satisfy our thirst for notice, to the fullest extent, from books of travel, as well as from the periodical press. Dr. John Howison, a Scotch traveller, tells the world of a people (meaning ourselves) "who are the untutored incorrigible beings that they were when, the ruffian remnant of a disbanded regiment or outlawed refuse of some European nation, they sought refuge in the wilds of Upper Canada, aware that they would neither find the means of sustenance, nor be countenanced in any civilized country." Sir Charles Dilke, in his "Greater Britain," pronounces Canadian loyalty to be mere hatred to the United States, and sees no reason why the Mother Country should spend blood and treasure in protecting Canadians against the consequences of their hate.* The *Edinburgh Review* describes us as "retainers who will neither give nor accept notice to quit." The Fenian raids evoked some plain language from a portion of the English press. One journal, the *Army and Navy Gazette*, said :—"There are upwards of 3,000,000 sturdy colonial Britons there, all told, and they are so dreadfully afraid of the approach of the raw, ragged Fenians that may succeed in forcing the United States *cordon*, as to be incessantly calling on the mother country for military aid. Every newspaper

* "Greater Britain," 4th Edition (1869), page 54.

in the colony is filled with the same doleful appeal for help. Canadians are calling lustily upon England to do for them what, if they had any pluck or spirit, they ought to do for themselves. They yield us no revenue, they give no encouragement to our trade, and yet, in the moment of assumed danger, they call out with almost feminine nervousness for help." One lady traveller, whose name is not vouchsafed to us, in the record of her experience in Canada, speaks of our most respectable society as being characterised by the manners of the kitchen, and the grotesque snobbery of the servants' hall. "Their ladies," says our waspish critic, "do not regard incivility as unladylike, and see little or no impropriety in rudeness, oftentimes mistaking the former for haughtiness, and supposing the latter to be the perquisite of good breeding."

Besides this direct method of toning our vanity, there is a sort of compliment and method of patronage that loses none of its sting by reason of indirectness. When Dr. McCaul deciphers obscure inscriptions, great wonder is expressed by foreign critics that so much sagacity and knowledge should ripen here; when Dr. Wilson writes of Pre-historic Man, amazement takes possession of the reviewer's breast; when Todd defines the limits of the royal prerogative and the theory and practice of parliamentary privilege, it is considered a remarkable circumstance that England should be indebted to a colonist for such a work; and even when a Canadian volunteer produces a book which is deemed worthy of translation into French and German, certain of the military authorities throw up their hands at such presumption, and point their satire with epithets whose force is supposed to lie

in certain equivocal associations connected with the word
" Colony " and the designation " Colonist."

A young country is peculiarly sensitive to outside
criticism. A very few words spoken in our favour, by a
stranger, give us pleasure; and a very few malicious
words, uttered to our detriment, irritate sorely. The fact
of being a dependent, though but in name, does not blunt
the edge of harshly-worded rebuke. Our cousins across
the lines, with all their self-esteem and resources, and
strength, smarted under the lash of a foreign press; so
that Canadians, with fewer pretensions, might be excused
for displaying somewhat of a similar weakness. It was
easy to laugh at us when, with pardonable vanity, we ex-
amined English opinion for some word of encouragement,
some tribute to our loyalty, some recognition of our industry, some acknowledgment of our progress. The
circumstances in which the various Provinces were placed
as well as the recollection of what had been endured in
the preservation of our allegiance, naturally enough
prompted us to look to the Mother Land for some appreciation of our steadiness of purpose. Little satisfaction was derived, by us at least, from the dictatorial
utterances, and still less from the scoldings indulged in,
with "all the license of ink," that came to us across the
ocean. We find, also, some ground of complaint in that
disregard of the tie of kinship and the bond of common
allegiance, which leads so many British travellers and
writers to lavish their compliments on the United States
and their satire on Canada. Time and again comparisons have been made to our prejudice in respect of progress. Time and again have we been lectured on our

bubbling and seething loyalty, and charged with an inclination to sponge on the Imperial exchequer. It is not difficult to ridicule hearty expressions of attachment, nor does it require great cleverness to fling off the word "lip-loyalty." Those who so glibly utter the reproach forget what it is that they are striking at. The citizen of the United States has a flag of his own and a nationality of his own—the Canadian has ever had to look abroad for his. For years British policy isolated the Provinces, to prevent their absorption in the neighbouring Republic, and in so doing stunted the growth of a native national sentiment. The exiles of the American Revolution carried hither the recollection of injuries endured and losses sustained, for a cause which they, foolishly or wisely, deemed worthy of the sacrifice. Many of them gave up home, lands, kindred, and the associations of youth, and exchanged comfort and ease for the dangers and hardships of an inhospitable and unknown wilderness. When Englishmen, therefore, undertake to cast reflections on a loyalty that has so frequently proved itself a reality, they should first consider how much is covered by the boast. Now that we are prosperous and united, vigorous and well-to-do ; and now that some of the traditions of the past are gradually losing their hold on the imagination of a new generation, that sentiment which so long found an outlet in declamation over the glories of the Mother Land, will draw a more natural nourishment from native sources. Critics should consider whether the doling out of so much gratitude for so much benefit received will be more acceptable than the hereditary romantic attachment which allowed no danger, no loss, no

neglect to sully its purity.   Young as we are, we are too
old to be abused without retort; weak as we may be,
we are too strong to be bullied with impunity.   What
we demand from English writers is fair play ; and should
the hour of peril come, we may venture to ask from
England, without sinking our self-respect, a quantum of
assistance proportioned rightly to the part we play in
attack or defence.   No decorations lavishly distributed,
no baronetcies generously conferred, can or will answer
as a substitute for respect and kindness or a mutual interchange of affection.*

As between the various Provinces comprising the
Dominion, we need some cement more binding than geo-

---

* The following extract from the *Church Herald*, the organ of the Church
of England in Canada, is worthy of serious consideration :—"Hereditary
honours may be suited to a country of hereditary estates.   But Canada is
not a country of hereditary estates ; nor is there, amongst our people, the
slightest tendency to make it so.   Consequently, if our leading men, instead
of being knighted, are made baronets, there will be some risk of our having
baronets sinking into the poorer classes of society, and trailing their
escutcheons in the dust.   Even in England, in spite of primogeniture and
family settlements, there is a considerable number of pauper peers, whose
titled indigence often forces them to sponge on the public, or resort to the
still lower expedient of marrying money-bags.   But in England the fortunes of the landed nobility and gentry are stability itself compared with
the perpetual fluctuations of Colonial wealth.   No doubt, in creating
Colonial baronets care will always be taken to select men so rich as to hold
out a fair hope of their transmitting large properties to their descendants.
But this will tend to another evil, inasmuch as it will lead the public mind
to connect honour with wealth, instead of connecting it with personal merit ;
and, assuredly, the lesson that wealth is above merit is not exactly the one
which commercial Colonies need to learn.

"There is another consideration which somewhat alloys our satisfaction
in seeing an English baronetcy conferred on a Canadian.   We regard with
jealousy on behalf of Canada anything which tends to make her leading
men look to another country, even though it be our mother country, for the
highest rewards of merit.   If Canada is to be a nation, it is time that her

graphical contact   some bond more uniting than a shift-
less expediency; some lodestar more potent than a mere
community of profit.   Temporizing makeshifts may suit
a futureless people.   Unless we intend to be mere hewers
of wood and drawers of water until the end, we should
in right earnest set about strengthening the foundations
of our identity; unless we are ready to become the
laughing-stock of the world, we had better not lose sight
of the awful possibility of sinking under self-imposed
burdens of territory.   It is not by mimicking the formali-
ties of the Old World, or aping time-worn solemnities
which have ceased to be solemn, that dignity is to be
acquired, nor is it by pantomime or burlesque that the

sons should begin to look for the highest rewards of merit here.   Hitherto,
the case of all the Colonies, in this respect, has been the same.   None of
them have been regarded, either by merchants or politicians, as their
country, the ultimate sphere of their own efforts and aspirations, and the
future home of their children.   The Colonial merchant has amassed wealth
in the hope of carrying it home to England, buying a great house in London, mingling as a member of the great plutocracy in London Society, and
rolling in a carriage round Hyde Park.   The politician, in the same manner, has looked for his highest meed, not to the applause of the Colony, or
to the gratitude of future generations of colonists, but to the favour of
Downing Street, and has trimmed his course in the hope of receiving the
rewards which Downing Street has to bestow, and of ultimately going home
to enjoy them.   While this continues it is impossible that we should have
truly national statesmen or chiefs of commerce and industry thoroughly
identified with our interests, present and future, and capable of the patriotic munificence which, it must be owned, nobly distinguishes the wealthy
men of the United States.   Canadian men will seek to leave their names
in the British peerage, not in the statute book of Canada; Canadian merchants, instead of spending their wealth in the acquisition of the renown
which belongs to the founders and benefactors of great national institutions,
will hoard it as a means of founding a family, and they will transfer it and
themselves as speedily as possible to the only country where a family can
be securely founded.   We prize as highly as it is possible to prize it, the continuance of an affectionate connection between Canada and the mother

thews of our nationality are to be strengthened. Peri-
wigs and Gold-sticks have had their day, and it is not
well for us to attempt to set up the mummied idols of a
buried past as objects of worship, or graft on our simple
Canadian maple the gaudy outgrowth of a luxuriant tro-
pical vegetation. Here, every man is the son of his own
works, and we need no antique code of etiquette nor the
musty rules of the Heralds' office to tell us whom or what
to honour.

We know not what the future may have in store for us.
Let the event be what it may, it is our bounden duty to
prepare for it like sensible men conscious of obligation to
humanity. The problem of self-government is being
worked out anew with fresh *data*, and we must do our

country; but the connection must be so regulated as not to prevent Canada
from becoming a nation.

"What we say with regard to the State in Canada, may be said with
regard to the Church also. We have sometimes heard complaints that the
merits of Colonial clergymen are not recognized by promotion in the English Church; but we cannot sympathize with these complaints, because it
appears to us that such promotion, however gratifying in some respects,
would confirm Colonial Churchmen in a misapprehension of their position.
Let the Church in Canada keep the most grateful recollection of her origin,
and cherish her spiritual connection with the Church of the mother country;
but she must remember that she is herself the Church, not of England, but
of Canada, and that she will have to draw her life from the soil in which
she is planted, and to adapt herself to the circumstances and exigencies of
her actual position. Our laity are apt to fancy that they are still members
of a Church established and endowed by the State, and to refuse to contribute for the support of the clergy to anything like the extent which the
voluntary system requires. Perhaps the clergy, on their part, sometimes
do a little to keep up this illusion. Both clergy and laity, however, must
get rid of it, if the Church is to prosper in this country. The Canadian
laity have to support a Canadian clergy under the voluntary system; the
clergy have to gain the confidence of the Canadian laity under the same
system, and to found the Church on the free allegiance of the Canadian
people."

part in the solution. There are asperities of race, of creed, of interest to be allayed, and a composite people to be rendered homogenous. Away down in Lunenburg, Nova Scotia, there is the old Teutonic stock, just as it exists in the county of Waterloo in Ontario; there are the descendants of the Pennsylvania Dutchmen in Lincoln, and of the New York Dutchmen around the Bay of Quinte; Highland Scotch clustering together in Prince Edward Island and Cape Breton, just as they do in Glengarry or Bruce; and the old Norman and Breton stocks in the Province of Quebec. In the interior of the continent there are French and Scotch half-breeds, with their Indian blood and Indian habits. Then again, across on the Pacific coast there is a motley collection of English, Irish, Scotch and Canadian, with all their varied peculiarities. But the task of fusing and blending these various elements is much less difficult than it seems. Switzerland has carried its constitution safely through three European revolutions, yet, of its two-and-a-half millions, one-and-two-thirds speak German, one-half million French, and the remainder Italian and other tongues. No;—the difficulty is not in the multitude of differences, real or fancied, that exists, but rather in finding some common basis of agreement strong enough to counteract disintegrating tendencies. Where are we to look for such a basis? In a work, lately published, an Englishman who paid us a visit, remarks that " to the Canadian it is of small concern what you think of his country. He has little of patriotic pride in it himself. Whatever pride of country a Canadian has, its object, for the most part, is outside of Canada." And the writer, from whom we are

quoting, goes on to assert that " whatever may be alleged
to the contrary, the belief in the possibility of a separate
future for Canada is steadily lessening among Canadians." Is this true? True or not, there is certainly some
ground to justify a casual visitor in such a conclusion.
We have too many among us who are ever ready to worship a foreign Baal, to the neglect of their own tutelary
gods. There are too many Cassandras in our midst; too
many who whimper over our supposed weakness and
exaggerate others' supposed strength. But there are
those who do not despair of the State; who are neither
weak-kneed nor faint of heart; who know that strength
comes from within. There is a name I would fain approach with befitting reverence, for it casts athwart
memory the shadow of all those qualities that man ad-
mires in man. It tells of one in whom the generous
enthusiasm of youth was but mellowed by the experience
of cultured manhood; of one who lavished the warm love
of an Irish heart on the land of his birth, yet gave a loyal
and true affection to the land of his adoption; who strove
with all the power of genius to convert the stagnant pool
of politics into a stream of living water; who dared to be
national in the face of provincial selfishness, and impar-
tially liberal in the teeth of sectarian strife; who from
Halifax to Sandwich sowed broadcast the seeds of a
higher national life, and with persuasive eloquence drew
us closer together as a people, pointing out to each what
was good in the other, wreathing our sympathies and
blending our hopes;—yes! one who breathed into our
New Dominion the spirit of a proud self-reliance, and
first taught Canadians to respect themselves. Was it a

wonder that a cry of agony rang throughout the land when murder, foul and most unnatural, drank the life-blood of Thomas D'Arcy McGee?

There are times when the sluggish pulse is quickened into activity; when the heart throbs with sympathy the most intense; when all that is human within us asserts unwonted supremacy. The sense of a loss shared in by each, of a danger encountered by all, brings before us with startling vividness how much we have in common. *Such a time it was* when the flower of our youth went forth to repel a wanton and unprovoked invasion. While tears sprang to the eyes of many fond fathers and loving mothers, affection itself was strengthened by the strain to which it became subject, and hallowed by the shrine of its self-immolation. *Such a time it was* when the lifeless bodies of those who fell in the conflict were brought home. Though a load of grief pressed on every heart, we felt proud that the post of danger had not been left to strangers; that bone of our bone and flesh of our flesh had been the first to meet the foe; that our own breasts had been bared to the storm. *Such a time it was* when the assassin's hand struck down the gifted, the genial, the patriotic McGee. Our country reeled with the blow. *Such a time it was* when the news of the butchery of young Scott at Fort Garry fell upon our ears, thrilling every nerve, and crowding the hot blood into our hearts. Humble though his position was—yet he was a Canadian; his mental gifts may have been few—yet he died for us. " *Spectet, inquit, patriam; in conspectu legum libertatisque moriatur. Non tu hoc loco Gavium non unum hominem, nescio quem, civem Ro-*

manum, sed communem libertatis et civitatis causam in illum cruciatum et crucem egisti." Let calumny do its worst—it shall not be said that the great statesman with brilliant talents and high place shall receive more abundant honour in his death than the poor friendless youth, who, away from kindred and home, cast all the attractions of life behind, and marched to his fate with a courage and devotion that fill us with awe. As we plant the cypress on the tenantless grave of the one unknown to fame save in his death, and wreathe with *immortelles* the headstone of an unpretending and almost friendless Canadian youth, we allow no inequality of mental gifts, no difference in position, to separate in our memory the orator and the statesman who dared to live for his country, and the brave yeoman who dared to die for it. Were he the most obscure in the land, were he without a friend in the wide world, the cause he died in was ours, and the consciousness of that sacrifice should make every Canadian his friend. There are those among us, God help them for cold-hearted sycophants! who dare to talk glibly of indiscretion when men have sacrificed the savings of a lifetime of toil, and mutter generalities about rashness when men have staked their lives. We have too little of that indiscretion and that rashness now-a-days. When we have grown so wise as to do everything by line and rule, and so discreet as to yield to the demands of force, we shall have attained a degree of perfection incompatible with a free existence. The meanest of all meanness is ingratitude, and there are degrees even in that. The thankless wretch who flings back in our teeth, alms, the measure of our ability, is a miracle of gratitude compared with him who seeks to blacken the memory of one who died a martyr, or, with malignant spite, to strip all of good from the sacrifice. We have need to stand by each other, and we would have all know that he who places us under national obligation shall not go unrewarded; that sufferings endured on our account shall not be forgotten; that the man who steps to the front shall neither be deserted nor harshly judged by those in the rear. We have been taunted with lack of confidence in the future of our country; let us not give occasion for the imputation of want of heart. It is alleged that we are prone to exhibit a cowardly spirit; let us show that we can at least recognize and respect courage.

We may, perhaps, lay ourselves open to the charge of sentimentalism, but men die for sentiment and oftentimes sacrifice everything for an idea. A piece of bunting is not of much worth, yet call it a flag and it may cost scores of lives; a song does not look very formidable, yet it may quicken revolution and desolate an empire. There is a national heart which can be stirred to its depths; a national imagination that can be aroused to a fervent glow; and when noble deeds are to be done, or great triumphs of progress and reform to be achieved, we appeal in vain to reason to lead the forlorn hope or mount the imminent deadly breach; but at the first trumpet-blast passion, enthusiasm, youth, step proudly to the front, and press forward with resistless, eager pace. The political machine must have a motive power; where shall we seek that power if not in the national character? A proper organization of those high qualities which form

character commends itself, therefore, as the elementary
work of those with whom the education of the people
rests. "You have sent your young men to guard your
frontier," said D'Arcy McGee. "You want a principle to
guard your young men; thus only can you guard your
frontier. When I can hear your young men say as proudly,
our federation, or *our* country, or *our* kingdom, as the
young men of other countries do speaking of their own, I
shall then have less apprehension for the result of whatever trials the future may have in store for us." The
safety of Troy depended upon the possession of the Palladium. Every people has its Palladium. Are we to be the
sole exception? stumbling forward we know not where!
groping for we know not what! only too glad to live on
sufferance! fully satisfied so long as we are permitted to
garner the weekly wage of toil! Do Canadians lack in
love of country? Search them out where you will—and
there is hardly a nook on the continent left unvisited by
their adventurous steps—and you find that change of
scene has neither obliterated nor tarnished the memories
which ever cling to the land of one's birth. Should danger threaten, we know that the thoughts of many a wan-
derer would turn towards his Northern home, and we
know, too, that no intervening distance, no fetter of self-
interest, would keep from our side, in the hour of trial,
the loyal and true sons of our common country.

Let but our statesmen do their duty, with the consciousness that all the elements which constitute greatness are now awaiting a closer combination : that all the
requirements of a higher national life are here available
for use; that nations do not spring Minerva-like into ex-

istence; that strength and weakness are relative terms, a few not being necessarily weak because they are few, nor a multitude necessarily strong because they are many; that hesitating, doubting, fearing, whining over supposed or even actual weakness, and conjuring up possible dangers, is not the true way to strengthen the foundations of our Dominion, or to give confidence in its continuance. Let each of us have faith in the rest, and cultivate a broad feeling of regard for mutual welfare, as being those who are building up a fabric that is destined to endure. Thus stimulated and thus strengthened by a common belief in a glorious future, and with a common watchword to give unity to thought and power to endeavour, we shall attain the fruition of our cherished hopes, and give our beloved country a proud position among the nations of the earth.

CANADA FIRST.

Address of the Canadian National Association to the People of Canada.

FELLOW COUNTRYMEN :

In addressing you thus early respecting a movement which has been successfully inaugurated in Toronto to promote the growth of a Canadian national sentiment and to secure Canadian unity, we recognize the necessity of freeing that movement from the effects of misconception as well as of wanton misconstruction. We had determined not to fetter the action or embarrass the deliberations of our Party convention (in which all the Provinces will be represented) by a premature declaration or any statement other than such as might be considered needful to indicate our objects in a general way. Our language must, therefore, be taken as expressive merely of local and individual opinion for which our friends outside of Toronto need not hold themselves responsible. As our motives have been impugned and systematic efforts are made to prejudice the public mind against us by distortion of our views and misstatement of our objects, we are forced for the sake of the movement whose success we have at heart to appeal directly to you. The misrepresentation to which we have alluded has, naturally enough, prompted many who sympathize with

CANADIAN NATIONAL ASSOCIATION.

49

the movement, and others who, while not in thorough
accord, are willing to judge it fairly, to ask for further
evidence as to our honesty of purpose, and further information as to our objects and plan of action.

Our motto, "CANADA FIRST," is said to admit of various interpetations—fertile imaginations have almost
proved that. Some profess to see in it, Annexation;
others, Independence; others, Know-nothingism. The
meaning attached to it by us may be gathered from the
following expressions of opinion, which will serve to show
that the motto is not necessarily ambiguous and has not
been misapprehended by all :—

"The germ of a national organization came to the surface during
the recent election in the capital of Ontario, with the watchword
'Canada First,' which is simply a declaration of patriotism."—
Canadian Monthly and National Review.

" Now, why should not this principle of nationality be applied
in Canada? There is more necessity for it here, at present, than
anywhere else we know of. It would unite the factions now tear-
ing themselves and the country to pieces, strengthen the weak
bonds which hold the Dominion together, elevate our statesmanship, give our young men something worth fighting for, and people
the country with a stream of immigration, now flowing into the
United States. It is said that encouraging this national spirit is
the surest way of hastening annexation to the United States, but
we say that nationality is the only sure preventive to annexation."
—*Canadian Nationalist.*

" Patriotism and loyalty are distinct, though they may at the
same time be agreeing sentiments. The one is devotion to one's
country; the other devotion to one's sovereignty; but there is no
need whatever for them to conflict with each other. The Englishman, while truly loyal to his Sovereign, gives his love of country
to England. The Scotchman and the Irishman while giving their

D

full allegiance to their Queen, give the first place in their affections to Scotland and Ireland. Why should we in Canada be different? What reason exists why when Englishmen, Irishmen and Scotchmen give their whole hearts to their respective countries, we in Canada should not place our own land first, and so act and speak as though we felt proud—as we have a right to be—of the name of Canadian. We have a country in which any people might glory, we have a future that is dazzling in its promise; all we need is a sentiment which shall break down all provincial and sectional distinctions, which shall make us feel not as Ontarions or Quebecers, Nova Scotians or New Brunswickers, but as Canadians—proud of our country as a whole."—*Hamilton Times.*

"And this is the feeling we want more of in our Dominion—a feeling of Canadianism. Are we to be forever jabbering about our respective merits as Englishmen, Scotchmen, Welshmen, French and Germans; as Irish Catholic and Irish Orangeman? We have heard a great deal too much of this stuff talked. It is time that all classes of our population, whether born here or elsewhere, whatever their creed or country, should consider themselves, above all, Canadians. It is from this standpoint that we bid God-speed to those who, in Toronto or elsewhere, are endeavouring to foster in our midst a national Canadian spirit."—*London Advertiser.*

"You want a principle to guard your young men, and thus only your frontier. When I can hear your young men say as proudly *our* federation, or *our* country, or *our* kingdom, as the young men of other countries do speaking of their own, I shall have less apprehension for the result of whatever trials the future may have in store for us."—*Thomas D'Arcy McGee.*

"They who hoped for a great future for this country, and who hoped to see its population largely increased, and knew that it had in it all the elements of becoming a great country, thought it necessary, in order to weld it together, that not only should they procure a teeming population, but that they should, most *continu-ously, deepen the interest of those who are already here.* Those who had settled here should join together in the earnest effort to wipe out provincial distinctions and internal dissensions. We must possess these elements of union if this is to be the country which we hope it is to be."—*Hon. Ed. Bloke, M.P.*

"It is Canada before any party ; the country before any faction."—*Thos. Moss, M.P.*

"There has been that in the history of Canada which rendered it absolutely necessary that all patriotic men, no matter of what creed or nationality, should band together for the purpose of checking the spread of that political fanaticism which has injured us so much in the past."—*Hon. M. C. Cameron.*

The signs of the times cannot be ignored, and whatever the future may have in store for us as a people, it is our duty to prepare for it like sensible men, conscious of the power which lies in massed strength, knowing our obligations and feeling their full weight, so much the more by reason of self-imposed burdens of territory.

The Empire is quite equal to the duty of self-care ; its interests will be best served by our doing, or trying to do, the best possible for ourselves, and the whole be best strengthened by giving strength to its weakest or supposed weakest part. Free government is a matter of compact, and, as such, involves reciprocal responsibilities which result in "virtual agreements, even as between he Imperial and Colonial Governments, respecting affairs mutually affecting them." If the power of veto implies mutual assent, and such agreements or assent admit of prior discussion, surely it is not improper for each of the contracting parties to urge its rights to its fullest extent no matter what the compromise result may be. In fact it is its duty so to do, and being such, when Canadian interests are made the subject of stipulation, it is natural and proper for Canada to give its best endeavours to advance them and secure justice. In the internal affairs there is no sufficient reason why the interests of Canadians should not be regarded when the interests of Canada are intertwined with them. For instance, in the management of our militia, the ambition and spirit of our volunteers have been thwarted and well-nigh destroyed by a pernicious system which prevails of *sacrificing the volunteer to the army officer*, no matter what the superiority of qualification in the former over the latter may be.' The consequence is seen in the rapid decay of our volunteer regiments.

It has been alleged that we desire to create antagonism between native born Canadians and Canadians by adoption. The contrary is the fact. Our earnest desire is to do away with all invidious distinctions of nationality, creed, locality or class, and to unite the people of the Dominion, as Canadians, through affection for and pride in Canada, their home. A serious impediment to our progress towards unity has been, and, unfortunately, still is, the hostility of *creed towards creed*, nationality towards nationality, class towards class, section towards section, which faction for its own selfish temporary purposes, provokes, and political sharpers systematically use. That hostility puts deep cutting weapons into the hands of the unscrupulous, and, though it may seem but to affect the unit, it has influenced the aggregate and tainted legislation.

It has been contended by some that our organization is but the advance-guard of Clear Gritism; by others that it is the Conservative party under a new name. Notwithstanding the certificates of character which some critics, with all the gravity of fortune-tellers, will thrust upon us in spite of protest, we form a new and distinct political organization for promoting, by a joint endeavour, the national interest upon a particular principle on which we are agreed. Owing to the relation Canada bears to the mother land, as a self-governing country, and the reciprocal obligations and responsibilities which that relation creates and implies, we consider it essential to our present, and still more so to our future, as a country, that the national heart be stirred, and the ennobling sentiments of which home and country is the source, be utilized to infuse into all the members of the Confederation the spirit of unity, vigour, self-reliance, and self-respect, as well as to give bent and impress to political action.

Principles should form the basis of party cohesion; not the memories of the past. A slavish clinging to the skirts of despotic individuals, with whom self is the all-in-all, should not be mistaken or substituted for manly support. Party, as a legislative instrument, should not be fastened to the chariot wheels of mere dictators, however able or troublesome, or made to serve as a yoke, under which all freedom of thought, independence of judgment and honesty of conviction must humbly and submissively pass, else except the penalty of black letter and ostracism. Public interests should not be subordinated to merely local or sectarian demands; nor power attained and held at the expense of honour and right. A spirit of calmness and judicial investigation should be brought to bear upon the discussion of public measures and the framing of laws, not that of subservient advocacy or dogged opposition. Honourable rivalry and the candid application of the rules of truth and justice should displace that virulence, slander and uncharitableness which characterize the bitter and ungenerous warfare of the two leading political parties in the press, on the hustings, and in Parliament. Such warfare has done much to disgrace the name of Canada abroad, and contributed greatly to the demoralization of our public men at home; has deterred from public life, or participation in politics, many of our worthiest and best; and has, by an incessant interchange of calumny and vituperation, confused the perceptions of the people, weakened their judgment, and well-nigh destroyed all belief in the existence of political morality.

Hence it is we arrive at the conclusion embodied in the resolution passed at the first public meeting of our party,

"That it is the duty of all Canadians whether such by birth or adoption to recognize the pressing necessity for the cultivation of a Canadian national sentiment which will unite the people of the various provinces more closely in the bonds of citizenship, promote a mutual confidence, whose common source of affection will prompt acts of toleration and words of respect, and prove the best safeguard for our Dominion against absorption on the one hand and disunion on the other."

The necessity for a new political party is manifest. Old party lines are obliterated; party nomenclature has become so diluted as to be almost incomprehensible, or at least incapable of intelligent explanation. The ins and outs cannot be segregated under the old names of Reformer and Conservative. Tory and Grit are merely synonymous with cat and dog, and convey no notion

save that of difference in momentum. If so in Ontario
and Quebec, how much more so in the other provinces,
where a helpless but contented ignorance prevails regarding the most cherished traditions of our dividing parties.
Seven years have elapsed since Confederation was accomplished, and to this day neither one nor other of our old
parties has established itself, as a party, in Nova Scotia,
New Brunswick, Manitoba, or British Columbia. Patronage and vituperation were equally inefficacious to give a
lasting foot-hold to either party, and to-day only too
many of the parliamentary representatives of these provinces, as well as of our own, think and act as mere delegates, while the patriotic sentiment of the various
provinces is left to draw a miserable sustenance from
geographical contact and the preamble to the Confederation Act.

There is a very large number of persons in even
Ontario and Quebec who acknowledge no allegiance to
either of the old parties and find no political body with
which they can act in concert. There are also many who
act at present with one or the other but desire a change.
It appears to us, therefore, that there is a large field for
a new party, and in the present dismembered and unsettled condition of those parties, which have hitherto
held sway, the present offers the most favourable opportunity for its establishment. Such a party, free from the
incubus of despotic repression and distasteful control,
unclogged with the weight of past misdeeds, based on
principles of a national character, capable of extension,
with equal facility into all parts of the Dominion, presenting an intelligible guarantee for united action, avail-
ing itself of the experience and prudence of age and

the energy and enthusiasm of youth, struggling honourably for success, and recognizing success only in the country's progress and the country's welfare—such a party, we say is possible, and given a stringent law to prevent bribery and corruption, vote by ballot to complete the severance of old party ties, income franchise to bring into play the energy, hopefulness, and self-devotion of the young men of Canada, we assert that such a party will be, and that its watchword, "Canada First," will, ere long, echo from the Atlantic to the Pacific. Unless we realize that, we shall have failed to accomplish our purpose. But we have no thought of failure. If such were entertained it could not survive the rapid increase of our organization, both here and elsewhere, the encouragement received from all parts of the Dominion, and the victory which attended our first active interference, as a party, in an election contest.

There is every indication that a newspaper will be established in Toronto in a short time, with such writing talent at its service as no journal in the Dominion can boast of; which, while it will not be the mere mouthpiece of any party, will yet do the Canadian National Party that justice which is denied it by any Toronto journal.

A club, under the auspices of the party, is now being founded in this city, which will combine the social, literary, and political elements, similar in plan to the English Reform or Carlton Clubs.

W. H. HOWLAND,
Chairman, pro tem.

W. G. McWILLIAMS,
Secretary, pro tem

ADDRESS TO THE

CANADIAN NATIONAL ASSOCIATION,

Delivered at Toronto, February, 1875.

IN the latter part of the year 1873 we met to give public expression to our political views. This was not done rashly or without a careful weighing of the consequences. We were comparatively few in number, and the leading journals made merry; we were not professional politicians, and the wirepullers and ward-politicians covered us with ridicule. We were persecuted by both Scribes and Pharisees. Some members of one of the old political factions pronounced us to be disguised Grits; by some of the other factions we were with equal confidence and equal vehemence set down as rank Tories. Each side showered epithets characteristic of its armoury, such epithets indeed as bear the same relation to the language of courtesy as the rude stone tomahawk does to the Damascened blade. The journalists and wirepullers of each side sought by an extravagant and distorted statement of our objects to prejudice public opinion against the movement, just as Demetrius the silversmith, and those whose living depended on the worship of Diana, excited commotion at Ephesus against the new doctrines of St. Paul. They felt their craft to be in danger. There were those among us who had acted with one of the old political parties; there were those who had been closely identified with the other; and there were also those who had theretofore taken no active part in politics. We had found, on consultation, that we were tired of the continual changes rung over extinct issues, and after a little mutual concession, discovered that a common ground existed on which all could unite. The conclusion arrived at was embodied in the following resolution :—

"That it is the duty of all Canadians, whether such by birth or adoption, to recognize the pressing necessity for the cultivation of a Canadian national sentiment, which will unite the people of the various Provinces more close-ly in the bonds of citizenship, promote a mutual confi-dence, whose common source of affection will prompt acts of toleration and words of respect, and prove the best safeguard for our Dominion against absorption on the one hand and disunion on the other."

The publishing of this was considered sufficient justifi-cation for dubbing us sentimentalists. " Canada First " was adopted as our motto (a self-assertive protest against party), and, forthwith, it became, according to our oppo-nents, a thing to be abhorred, and we were dragged into unpleasant notoriety as know-nothings, annexationists, independence men, and traitors. We pointed out that the dividing lines between the old parties had been obliterated, so far as either principle or practice was concerned, that on the one side, antipathy to Mr. George

Brown and the *Globe* constituted the sum total of characterizing principle, if such it can be called; while, on the other, a hatred of Sir John A. Macdonald, and an awe of Mr. Brown, were the zenith and nadir of party thought; that on the strength of such differences, people were asked and expected to surrender the fee simple of their judgments to a daily newspaper, to mortgage their consciences for the benefit of wire-pulled conventions, and to sacrifice everything characteristic of national manhood to the Moloch of Party. We showed that neither of the parties, Grit or Tory, had obtained a foothold in the Provinces outside of Ontario and Quebec, and that the representatives of Nova Scotia and New Brunswick, Manitoba and British Columbia were forced to engage in parliamentary contests which had no interest for them save in speculation as to the probable vanquished, or in nice calculations as to the bleeding power of the victor. Their politics were, and perhaps still are, " better terms." The contract of Confederation was being opened afresh every few days, and its scarcely cicatrized wounds pleaded piteously for rest. We were taunted, in reply, with wishing to play at straddle-the-fence in politics—which to the mind of the sycophantic partisan is a terrible crime, and to the convention-monger an unpardonable sin. It was all right for a Party to balance expediencies, to make open questions, and even to veer about from extreme to extreme, but for an individual to pause and reflect, to take a dispassionate view of both sides prior to coming to a conclusion, to speak as his judgment dictated, and to vote as his conscience approved, was to become a pervert to that greatest heresy of orthodox party politics, otherwise called Independence. We insisted that Party had become faction ; that wrangling had taken the place of debate ; that the respectable and thinking classes were ceasing to vote ; that the difficulty of finding men of integrity and worth to accept political positions had been intensified to an alarming degree by party violence and individual despotism : that personal abuse and recrimination had well-nigh destroyed the people's faith in their public men, and that even the newspaper had become, by reason of its vituperative vocabulary, a dangerous guest at the fireside. Party strife had been carried to such lengths that no one of sagacity placed the slightest reliance on a newspaper report of a speech, or read leading articles for any other purpose than that of keeping abreast of the fictions of the period. This provoked from the *Mail* the contemptuous retort, "beardless boys," and from the *Globe* the equally withering phrase, "sucking politicians." We were prepared for that method of attack, and made due allowance for an exuberance of senile wit on the part of those who gibbered behind the palings of Faction. Conscious that we could not be laughed out of existence in such innocent displays of humour, we directed our attention to the removal of the doubt and suspicion as to our motives and objects, which misrepresentation had begotten in the minds of many who, weary of party strife, and dissatisfied with existing combinations, longed for a change, and were willing to assist in bringing it about. We were asked for a detailed statement of principles. The reason for our being was apparent to all save heated partizans.

But, it was asked, what practical good did we expect to accomplish and how did we purpose to proceed? These inquiries resulted in an Address which our Association issued and scattered broadcast over the country. In this our platform was set forth in detail, and after the lapse of fourteen months, I think none of us have reason to feel ashamed of it. It included, as you remember, consolidation of the Empire, and in the meantime a voice in the making of treaties affecting Canada; Income Franchise; the Ballot, with the addition of compulsory voting; a scheme for the representation of minorities; the reorganization of the Senate; an improved Militia System under the command of trained Dominion officers. The enunciation of these as definite objects of united action threw the leading journals into ecstasies of wrath. The "sucking politicians" having gone through the sentimental stage had at length revealed themselves as hair-brained theorists! "Every one of these planks," exclaimed the *Globe*, "is calculated to inspire sensible men with wonder, if not with ridicule and contempt." "The innocent work of bumptious lads who have not cut their eye-teeth in politics," cried the *Mail*. "Nothing but windy and meaningless utterances," shouted a third journalist. Even the *Leader*, catching the prevailing mania for strong language, though but half awake, called out lustily "sucking traitors," to the great consternation of many of Mrs. Gamp's family. Disregarding the infirmities of its nervous readers, it even went so far as to tell them abruptly that "the real motives of the sect (!) are Anti-British and Yankee," and that we were but "a new fang for the mouth of the Grit serpent through which to pour his venom into the bodies of his opponents." Fired by the seeming universality of the chorus, Mr. M. C. Cameron assured the public that " he was not prepared to retire in favour of these young gentlemen," " but more likely to prepare a dish of pap for these boys." He, of course, is excusable. He always plays Rip Van Winkle well. The last shot of this campaign of humour was fired by the *Globe*. It called our platform " piebald " and its details " a bundle of incongruous planks."

The tactics which had dictated ridicule first, and wholesale condemnation afterwards, were found ineffectual either to destroy our zeal, check the growth of our organization, or prevent investigation. So there was a change of front. The minority question was taken up and demolished in one article. The Senate reform was pronounced absurd, and compulsory voting shared the same fate ! This was done on the plan by which history, geography and political economy are taught in one lesson in quack schools. The public discussion which ensued, shallow as it was, feeble and unscholarly though it was, attracted attention, and it soon became confessed that the National Party had given journalists something to think about, to read about, and to write about ; had placed before them questions which demanded some qualities of mind other than those necessary to perfection in invective, and an acquaintance with books and political systems more extensive than that required for putting down a ward politician, or reviewing a Parliamentary debate, or the fence around the Front Street buildings, or even defending the Ontario Government for the purchase of a $5 chromo. It was noised about throughout the land that subjects for political discussion had come to the surface which were worthy of examination, and that these men, possessing claims to education (I speak of those on the roll of our Association), and holding not unworthy positions in their respective spheres, who, undeterred by the scoffs of the ignorant or the sneers of the overwise, were neither ashamed nor afraid to call themselves independent in politics.

But times have changed somewhat, and as we look back we can afford to be amused at the vain efforts of our critics and the ineffectual labours of our opponents. The name and motto of our organization have gone through the length and breadth of Canada, and, here and there, we can point to spots where both have taken firm root and defy extirpation. The sentiment of Nationality has revealed itself a living force, snapping the fetters of Party; giving voice and direction to aspirations which hitherto struggled in vain for utterance; placing in the hands of the weak a powerful weapon of defence, and in those of the strong an arm effective in attack; utilizing for the public good the enthusiasm of youth and the experience of age; and, by supplying evidence of its cohesive qualities, bringing home to our public men in all plainness the fact that the time has arrived for recognizing the existence of Canada as a country having a hold upon the affections of its people, and that all the resources which the magic words "home and country" place at their disposal, might, and should be mined to better purpose than that of forging self or playing the pander to Party. It may be well for "practical politicians" to attempt to moderate enthusiasm by twitting us with sentimentalism ; but they should remember that the germ of all revolutions in politics is sentiment. That national sentiment has commended itself to some of our leading public men is pleasant to reflect upon, and that they now dare to speak of it is satisfactory. Although the *Globe* told us that "it may tickle the ears of the groundlings to cry that there is no principle so heart-stirring as Nationality," Lord Dufferin did not hesitate to say " there is no feeling by which the Canadian people are animated with which I sympathize more than in their desire to build up their country into a distinct, prosperous and respected nationality," and again, " I am happy to see in every Province and locality I have visited, the time has come for laying aside sectional distinctions, and for combining one grand effort to create a nationality that shall know no distinction from the Atlantic to the Pacific Ocean." Mr. Blake was equally outspoken and emphatic. " The future of Canada, I believe, depends very largely upon the cultivation of a national spirit. We must find some common ground on which to unite, some common aspiration to be shared, and I think it can be alone found in the cultivation of that spirit." I might give many more extracts to prove that a chord has been struck which vibrates with a clear, distinct and delicious harmony. But to be convinced of that you need only read the speeches now delivered by men of any pretension to prominence among Canadians, and compare the references to Canada's progress and Canada's future with the wails of olden time when faith in our country's continued existence was kept as a secret too childish or too extravagant for confession, and aspirations towards nationality

too chimerical and quixotic to find a place in our literature. Were Thomas D'Arcy McGee alive to-day he would
find that the seeds which he scattered broadcast through
the land and watered with his blood, have yielded a
rich harvest.

Our newspapers have taken shame to themselves for
outraging the public sense of fairness, and disregarding
the amenities and courtesies of honourable controversy.
The *Globe* has risen to explain, and the *Mail* has attempted to clear its skirts. It is true each has cast the
blame upon the other ; but the very fact that excuse has
been deemed necessary, may be fairly claimed as a tribute to the ameliorating influences of our movement. It
must not be forgotten that there was something to be
said on behalf of the offending journals. They were
striving to rebuild party walls, not only without bricks,
but also without straw for the bricks. Principles were
not available for the creation of broad distinctions: hence
the only means of perpetuating Grit and Tory, as such,
was to fan the flame of personal animosity and frown
down philosophical speculation. But the newspapers,
with all their power, have had to give way, and are now
engaged in the laudable task of fortifying their minds
with facts relative to the much despised abstractions,
and furbishing up arguments for or against the much
ridiculed incongruities.

That journals have exercised and do still exercise
great influence over the people of this country is un-
questionable ; but growing intelligence not only demands
that appeals to evil passions be exchanged for appeals to
reason, that abuse give way before argument, but has

E

already begotten a competition which is fraught with great good. The fact that *The Liberal* can establish itself alongside three daily newspapers in a city of 60,-000 people, demonstrates that there is a craving for a new state of things in our periodical literature. If that journal makes the mistake of supposing that mere organs are wanted here, such mistake will prove fatal. Its success will depend on the character for boldness and independence it must earn.

In October last, Mr. Blake—one gifted with the power of analysis beyond those of any of our public men, a great lawyer and an accomplished speaker, a Saul among our statesmen, a Samson among our politicians, an Achilles among our debaters, and last, though not least, a man in whose honour all believe, in whose integrity none lack faith—spoke out his mind at Aurora, to the consternation, as may be imagined, of his congregation of convention-mongers, wirepullers and local politicians. Horror took possession of their souls. Here was a man daring to think for himself. What would the party say ? Here was a man daring to utter heresy, " We must find some common ground on which to unite, some common aspiration to be shared, and I think it can be alone found in the cultivation of a national spirit." In fact, in the words of the *Globe*, tickling the ears of the groundlings ! Here was a man daring to criticise the critics by exploding the notion that the cultivation of that sentiment involved the practical advocacy of Annexation ! Here was a a man daring to say "the time will come when that national spirit will be truly felt amongst us, when we shall realize that we are four millions of people who are not free,

when we shall be ready to take up that freedom and to
ask our share of national rights!" Here was a man ad-
vocating a reconstruction of the Senate, compulsory voting, and a scheme for the representation of minorities!
What would the *Globe*, the Alpha and Omega of the Grit
party, say to all that? No wonder the nervous trembled
and held their breath. When these principles were
enunciated by us the *Globe* had said that they were calculated to inspire sensible men with wonder, if not with
ridicule and contempt. What was then said of us all
know. However, the *Globe* attacked Mr. Blake with a
boomerang, doubtless because it was impolitic to deal
him direct blows. It shot at him around corners. Ourselves and Mr. Goldwin Smith, who was absent from
Canada when our Association and the National Club
were formed, came in for a good share of its attentions.
But its tone was changed. It took off the mask of Momus.
The light and airy style was abandoned for the heavy
tragic, and the "innocent absurdity" of yesterday, yclept
the Canada First Party, became with it a formidable conspiracy, contemplating "action at once aggressive and
dangerous."

> *Et jam prima novo spargebat lumine terras*
> *Tithoni croceum linquens Aurora cubile.*

During the session before last of the Ontario Legislature, the principle of compulsory voting was brought before that body, at the instance of Mr. Bethune, and during the last session it came up for discussion. The
speech of Mr. Bethune, who, you will remember, has had
large experience in election matters, was one that com-

manded universal approbation and convinced many who had been skeptical. I am not called upon here to recapitulate his arguments, but when you find such men as Mr. Bethune, Mr. S. C. Wood, Mr. Deroche, and last, though not least, our patronising Rip Van Winkle, Mr. M. C. Cameron, giving in his adhesion to it, you may recall with complacency the explosion of laughter with which it was greeted when we first ventured to assume its advocacy as a practical reform. Had Mr. Bethune pressed for a vote in the House, the principle of compulsory voting would have been adopted then and there. The converts to the principle, outside the House, may, since the last elections, be numbered by thousands, and we may now look forward to the early placing on the Statute Book of Ontario of a law compelling voters to fulfil their trust. In the Dominion Legislature, resolutions affirming the principle were introduced last session and will doubtless be again brought forward during the current one.

When we announced, as part of our programme, a scheme for the representation of minorities, one leading journal treated it with the loftiest scorn as being impracticable and useless, but when we recollected that the proposition to give minorities an equal representation was being advocated in France and Germany, in New South Wales and Victoria, that a scheme having that object in view was in actual operation in Denmark, in England, in Illinois, and in Pennsylvania, we took courage. When we read Mr. J. S. Mill's opinion that Hare's plan " has the almost unparalleled merit of carrying out a great principle of government in a manner approaching to ideal perfection as regards the special object in view" we grew bolder; and when we looked into the political statistics of our country, noted the peculiarities of our position as regards creeds, commercial interests and nationalities, we became convinced that a change in our plan of representation was a palpable necessity. The expediencies which obtain in our politics have been of late years a fruitful source of demoralization to our representatives. They have had to be all things to all men, and offensive in word or act to none. Selected for availability, *i.e.*, having done nothing that could be taken hold of by opponents, or, on account of pure sycophancy, they are plunged into an election contest with the advice ringing in their ears, "Take care, don't commit yourself." In their speeches they keep themselves tight hauled and sail close to the wind. In fact, the model politician, according to party, is a man as full of tricks as a fox, quick in prevarication and schooled never to put his head so far into a hole as not to be able to slip it out at a moment's notice. Such an exemplar produces general slipperiness, oiliness, and hypocrisy. Honest earnestness goes to the wall and outspoken conviction ensures defeat. The representation of minorities would, we think, check all that. Take the case of the late alliance between the Catholics and the Clear Grits. The Catholics wished for representation and some of the astute wirepullers among the Grits arranged an alliance. If you support Mr. Crooks we will support Mr. O'Donohoe, was said. Each doubted the other, and the result was as might have been anticipated. Now, had the Catholics a system under which they could have elected a man of their choice without going under obligations to others, and had candidates been put forward for the Grits to vote for without the incubus of an enforced alliance? If the result would not have answered expectations, it would at least have prevented a deal of post mortem recrimination and dislike. I do not mean to say that it would be well to have Catholic representatives or Protestant representatives merely as such; but if creed will not be content without a representation in Parliament, let it elect its candidate fairly if it can, without forcing a person to vote in favour of a person he dislikes, or against those whom he prefers. There is a variety of plans before us to select from; the Cumulative Vote, which entitles every elector to a number of votes equal to the number of members to be chosen, and gives him the right to cast all his votes for one candidate or distribute them among the candidates as he thinks fit. As if Toronto were one constituency, returning three members (instead of, as it is, three constituencies with three members), and each elector had three votes. Under this cumulative plan he might give three votes to one candidate, or one vote to each of the three. This plan obtains in Illinois. The restricted vote would with Toronto returning three members, limit each elector to two votes, so that a minority of two-fifths of the constituency would return one member. The Hare plan is far more elaborate. It would throw the whole country into one constituency, divided into a certain number of quotas, entitled to a representative. As if the whole number of voters was 30,000, and the number of members to be elected thirty, each thousand voters would have a representative. Under it a voter in

Toronto could cast his vote for a candidate in Halifax or Montreal, or any other place, and *vice versa*. Under Mr. Hare's plan each candidate for the representation of any constituency could send his name to an officer, called the Registrar General, who would publish the names of all the candidates.   The mode of voting is that each ballot may contain the names of more than one person as the elector chooses.   Each candidate has counted in his favour the number necessary to make up his quota, and the remaining voting papers in which the name of such candidate appears at the head of the list are appropriated to those who are the voter's second choice.   For instance, an elector votes for A first, B second, C third, &c.   In case A has received more than enough votes to elect him, the remainder is carried to the credit of B, who benefits by that excess as well as by the direct votes in his favour. The sum and substance of the plan is: A votes for B, C, and D.   If A has enough to elect him, B reaps the overplus; and if C, then D's turn comes.   The advantages gained from the method of voting under this plan are claimed to be, that it protects the minority from the tyranny of the majority, and minority and majority alike from the tyranny of party chiefs; permits the utmost freedom of individual action; gives every representative a constituency who are unanimous in his support; makes it for the interest of every party to put forward its best men, and makes it worth while for good men to come forward as candidates, and affords intelligence free choice. Of all countries, Canada and the United States stand most in need of minority representation, owing to the extent to which log-rolling, gerrymandering, canvassing.

and wirepulling are carried on, not to speak of the vindictiveness of party spirit. Mr. Blake's views on the subject were expressed as follows :—

" I believe we might effect immense improvements upon the present system of popular representation. For my own part, I have been for some time dissatisfied with our present mode of popular representation, as furnishing no fair indication of the opinions of the country. I do not think a system under which a majority in one consti- tuency elects a member, the minority being hopeless, helpless, without any representation at all of its own, is a good system. I have been collecting some statistics on this subject, and it is extraordinary to what extent the popular voice, as shown in the popular vote, differs from the expression of that voice in the Legislature. In Nova Sco- tia, in the year 1867, there was a bitterly-fought contest on the question of Union or anti-Union. The result was that only Mr. Tupper was returned from the whole Pro- vince, and that by a very narrow majority, as a repre- sentative of the Union sentiment. I have analyzed the statistics of that election, and I find that the real strength exhibited at the polls would have given, as nearly as I can estimate, seven to the Union side instead of one, and only twelve to the anti-Unionists instead of eighteen. Take Nova Scotia again in 1874. The returns gave nine- teen to the Government, one Independent, and one Op- position. The popular vote on that occasion would, as nearly as I can judge, have given eight out of twenty-one to that side instead of two, and but thirteen to the Gov- ernment instead of nineteen. Our principle of govern- ment is that the majority must decide. Upon what is it founded ? Well, you cannot give a reason except this, that it is necessary. It is the only way in which government can be carried on at all. But if the minority must, on this ground of necessity, bow to the voice of the majority, the majority is all the more bound to see that the minority has its fair share of representation, its fair weight in the councils of the country. The majority must recollect that it may become the minority one day, and that then it would like to have its fair share in those councils, and such disparities as these are not likely to induce a feeling of cheerful submission on the part of the minority of Ontario, in the elections of 1867. I cannot, of course, be precisely accurate in these matters, because there were some acclamation returns, and there are other difficulties in making an exact calculation—but there were eighty-two members to be returned. The whole popular vote would have resulted in a slight majority for the Liberal party over the Government, but, discarding fractions, the result would give forty-one members to each. The Government, however, carried forty-nine seats to thirty-three, and so the Liberal party did not obtain its fair share in the government of the country. A turn of 408 votes would have taken seventeen seats from the Government and given them to the Liberal party. In the late election of 1874, the popular voice, although very strongly in favour of the Government, was by no means so decided as the returns showed. And besides this, 178 votes turned the other way would have changed eight seats, making a difference of sixteen on a division. Little more than double that number would have changed sixteen seats, or thirty-two on a division, and this in a

Province where over 200,000 votes would, if all the elections were contested, have been polled. I represent a constituency in which many more votes were polled against me than sufficed to return Mr. Dymond. Within nine of 2,000 votes were polled against me. Can I say I represent those people? I do not. I do not represent their views. They thought I was wrong, they wished to defeat me, they wished to condone the Pacific Scandal and to support the late Government. I am bound to consider their individual wants, but I cannot say I represent their views. How are they represented? Some will say that people a long way off elected, say, Mr. Cameron, of Cardwell, or Mr. Farrow, of North Huron, to represent them. That is a peculiar mode of representation by which the unrepresented minorities of adverse views in different constituencies are in effect told that they are to be content because there are others in the like evil plight. Look at home. Take, if you please, the old County of York, including Toronto, Ontario, and Peel. You have there nine districts, and you have nine members all on one side, and not a single one on the other. The popular vote gave you five and your adversaries four, and upon a proper system of representation that would have been the proportion of the members."

I prefer the Hare plan, and would like to have tried the experiment of electing the Senate in accordance with it. The question of reorganizing the Senate is one on which all Reformers are now pretty much agreed, and Mr. Mills, who has made the subject his own, stands manfully to his annual resolution in the Dominion Legislature. He advocates a Senate elected by the local Legislatures.

I do not object to that in default of anything better. But I consider that the Senate should be in part elective and in part non-elective. The elective portion should be selected upon Hare's plan, and the non-elective portion made up of Lieut.-Governors, ex-Premiers, Judges of the Superior Courts, who have completed their term of office, &c. The non-elective part of the Senate would thus be composed of life members of experience, character, and standing; and the elective part would comprise a class whose election under the Hare plan would be a guarantee of fitness and ability. We have too little culture and worth in the country to squander it, and there is no good reason why we should not have the means of rewarding, or, not to speak of utilizing, the experience of such men as the late Robert Baldwin, or Chief Justice Draper (I use them as cases in point), for a lifetime spent in the service of Canada, without resort to titles and decorations unsuited to the genius of our people, and not much valued where they are more in consonance with prevailing ideas.

It may be asked why we did not avail ourselves of the late elections to put our principles to the test of the ballot box. The chief reason is only too evident—the Act giving an Income Franchise, by some curious contrivance, did not come into force until it was too late, and many farmers' sons are still without votes. Our strength, as yet, lies among the young men. But we have taken a hand in elections, and Toronto East and West bear witness to what "Canada First" can do. Mr. S₁ohn polled a large vote in one of the Wentworths, and that without assistance—without conventions or wirepullers. Had Dr. Devlin not resigned, it is said he would have run well.

However, we knew our time had not arrived for successful encounter with the two old parties, with their organizations and advantages, and no object was to be gained by bringing out candidates under the circumstances, for the sake of incurring defeat.

The elections of the Local Legislature were, for obvious reasons, converted by the Government into a party struggle, and when political discussion did not draw largely from the Pacific Scandal and old-time corruptions, it flamed up over little Mrs. Blank, the fence around the Parliament Buildings, or the alleged pranks at the Model Farm. The Opposition was very small—according to the Government organs ridiculously small—so small, indeed, as to fall far below "the strong and healthy" Opposition which is the delight of the advocates of party when in the height of an argument upon the advantages of party government. The Conservative, or, as some say, the Tory Party, felt itself in the last ditch. Without leaders in whom it could trust, its most prominent men, persons whom it despised ; its colours trailed through the dust by those whose duty it was to have preserved them honoured and unsullied ; its war cries changed for ear-piercing abuse, stolen from the back numbers of Clear Grit newspapers, and adapted to the occasion ; so led and so armed this once great political party waged an unequal, hopeless guerilla warfare in its graveclothes. Its opponents, strong in numbers, conscious of swaying the influence of two governments, went to the polls with the confidence which being " in " gives as against those who are " out." But though party could fight its way to the polling booth, the aperture in the ballot-box was rather small for its forged proportions. And though Grit and Conservative may claim this victory or that defeat as the result of party conflict, one may safely aver that personal qualifications and local influences, altogether apart from politics, had much to do with the result.

I think I have made it plain that our movement has not been unattended with some good effects, and that we have no reason to feel ashamed of the progress made by the principles we coalesced upon. That movement was at the outset, as has been well said by a recent reviewer, "an intellectual movement." "It was," he goes on to say, "the revolt of educated and thoughtful men against the inanity, and worse than inanity, of what was offered to them as political discussion. It was a direct product, in some measure, of that higher culture which the universities and colleges of our land are steadily promoting." It was not devised for the mere sake of agitation, and though we are appealed to by the *Globe*, in its newest Tory *rôle*, to rest and be thankful for what is, we feel that this, by reason of its youth and elasticity, is the country for political experiment, and we know that government being for the good of the governed, it is our duty to the world at large, as well as to ourselves, as feeling that the details of our system are not perfect; as being of those to whom representative institutions have been happily granted to carry on the work of reform, to do our part in the solution of the problem of self-government, and be able to render a good account of our trust. Can that be accomplished by standing still when there is so much work to be done ? by refusing to discuss principles, howsoever new, or by continuously ringing changes on past events, howsoever old ? In local affairs we have a municipal system which is robbing the people right and left by giving power to rings and small groups of individuals to levy taxes without end on the community. Officials are multiplying in triplets. Faction has gripped the throat of our City Councils, County Councils, and Local Legislature. These and numerous other questions are calling lustily for reform. So far as we are concerned, however, we have received every encouragement to further effort. "The giants of party warfare," says a critic, "laughed to scorn at first the striplings, as they deemed them, who stood forth and challenged them to combat; but more than one well-directed pebble has smitten the forehead of the boasters and given them cause at least for serious and painful feeling." No later than a week or two ago, Mr. M. C. Cameron, who had, as we have before seen, expressed himself so scornfully of us, treated the Conservatives assembled at dinner at Barrie, to the piece of information that "Our party, though small, was composed of men of culture and position." The fact is, we have achieved a triumph over self-interested and hireling partizanship second only to that won over ignorance and inertness. That such triumph allowed the exercise of honourable and fair means is not the bitterest ingredient in our cup of rejoicing.

With such a past it is not unnatural to ask ourselves, what of the future ? National sentiment is steadily growing in Canada, but much remains to be done to carry it beyond the boundaries of the cities and villages into the farm house and the shanty. Much remains to be done to convince the obtuse and the suspicious (owing to the misrepresentation of which our motives have been the subject) that when we say Canada First we don't mean Canadians first. We are not such fools as to suppose that a Canadian is better than anybody else, or is entitled as such to a preference over anybody else. We have no longing for a schedule of disabilities. But at the same time many of us think a Canadian is no worse than other people, and we would have all who have made Canada their home, feel or try to feel that there is no disgrace attached to the name Canadian, and that to be known as such, either here or abroad, involves no social or political obstruction. The great lesson to be learned after all is, as D'Arcy McGee taught, to learn to respect ourselves, to have a modest but firm confidence in our own strength, and an equally certain hope in our future. Some say such expressions point to annexation. If we, and most of us, happen to be sons of the soil,—are annexationists, who are the loyal men? Our idea has always been that it is only by deepening faith in Canada, our home and country, that we as a people can hope to exist separate and distinct. De Tocqueville, in his book on America, said the United States had no neighbours. An English writer, a short time ago, stated that " Whatever pride of country a Canadian has, its object for the most part is outside of Canada, and the belief in the possibility of a separate future for Canada is steadily lessening among Canadians." I am sure that this is untrue, but I am equally sure that there is some ground to justify a casual visitor in such a statement. We have transplanted from Ireland a feud which seems

to have crossed the Atlantic only for the purpose of
securing greater freedom of action, without leaving behind a shred of its malignity and bitterness, and thus are
forced among us causes of discord which dictate and defy
legislation, and, wedge-like, divide large sections of the
community into unreasoning antagonism.   There is one
consolation, however, which Mr. N. F. Davin, in a letter
to the editor of a Catholic newspaper, has forcibly pointed out, namely, that, " at present both Irish Orangemen
and Irish Roman Catholics are practically placed outside
all positions of place and power," thanks to the faction
fights of Orange and Green.   His conclusion is just as
ours has been, " in favour of the general comprehensive
policy of being Canadians first, and seeking honestly to
meet the problem of the present and the future, which
are presented by a people drawn from different countries,
and of different faiths in the process of becoming homo-
geneous."

It has also been charged against us that we are advocates of the dismemberment of the Empire.   Curiously
enough, complaints on this score have come chiefly from
the organs of the political parties that uttered no moan
when Sir Alexander Galt, Mr. Huntington, Mr. Holton,
and others preached immediate Independence.   The fact is
we no more advocate independence than we advocate the
day of judgment.   There are those among us who think
just as Mr. Gladstone, Mr. Bright, Mr. Lowe, Mr. Brown,
Sir Alexander Galt, Mr. Blake and others think, that the
relations of Canada to the Empire are proper subjects for
discussion ; that some day or other separation may or
must come, and that now is the time to at least begin to

prepare for it. England has been trying for years to make us stand upon our feet. The troops have been withdrawn. We are allowed to legislate as we please, and there is great dislike to interfere with our action. It would rather take us aback if at some early day we were made to strike out for ourselves without any preparation for the event. What must come is either a Federation of the Empire or Independence. I think I cannot do better than quote to you the language of Mr. Blake :

" Matters cannot drift much longer as they have drifted hitherto. The Treaty of Washington produced a very profound impression throughout this country. It produced a feeling that at no distant period the people of Canada would desire that they should have some greater share of control than they now have in the management of foreign affairs ; that our Government should not present the anomaly which it now presents—a Government the freest, perhaps the most democratic, in the world with reference to local and domestic affairs, in which you rule yourselves as fully as any people in the world, while in your foreign affairs, your relations with other countries, whether peaceful or warlike, commercial or financial, or otherwise, you have no more voice than the people of Japan. This, however, is a state of things of which you have no right to complain, because so long as you do not choose to undertake the responsibilities and burdens which attach to some share of control in these affairs, you cannot fully claim the rights and privileges of free-born Britons in such matters. But how long is this talk in the newspapers and elsewhere, this talk which I find in

F

very high places, of the desirability, ay, of the necessity
of fostering a national spirit among the people of Canada
to be mere talk ?   It is impossible to foster a national
spirit unless you have national interests to attend to, or
among people who do not choose to undertake the responsibilities and to devote themselves to the duties to
which national attributes belong.   It is for us to determine—not now, not this year, not perhaps during this
Parliamentary term, but, yet, at no distant day—what
our line shall be.   For my part, I believe that while it
was not unnatural, not unreasonable, pending that process of development which has been going on in our new
and sparsely-settled country, that we should have been
quite willing—we so few in numbers, so busied in our
local concerns, so engaged in subduing the earth and
settling up the country—to leave the cares and privileges
to which I have referred in the hands of the parent
State ; the time will come when that national spirit
which has been spoken of will be truly felt among us,
when we shall realize *that we are four millions of Britons who are not free,* when we shall be ready to take
up that freedom and to ask what the late Prime Minister
of England assured us we should not be denied—our
share of national rights."

So that after all the hysterics into which the super-
heated loyalists were thrown, we think that their frantic
outcries over the safety of the Empire were but "windy
suspirations of forced breath."   We think that the Empire is quite strong enough to take care of itself, and that
what English statesmen desire us to do is to strengthen
ourselves in every possible way.   They would be better

pleased by our exhibiting signs of vigour and life than if
we were to send reams of platitudes to the foot of the
throne, or wake the echoes with mouthing loyalty.
D'Arcy McGee well said, " When I can hear our young
men say as proudly *our* federation, or *our* country, or
our kingdom, as the young men of other countries do
speaking of their own, I shall then have less apprehension for the result of whatever trials the future may have
in store for us." There is a loyalty in which we lack,
and that is loyalty to ourselves. No wonder. From the
top to the bottom of our majority system of government
there is so little independence of mind and real freedom
of discussion on the part of public men and journalists
as to make one feel a degree of shame. Opinion halts
timidly and cowers at its own shadow. We stand greatly in need of statesmen with backbone—men who will
take positions and not fear to tell us so—men who will
think for themselves, judge for themselves, and act in
accordance with their own conviction, neither driven
into the rut of casuistry by concealed enmity, nor into
devious ways by open defiance. For taking an open and
manly stand, Mr. Goldwin Smith (partly on our account
and partly on his own) has been made a target for all the
arrows left in the quivers of partisan journalists. However, they must needs furnish themselves with a fresh
supply, as I fancy the target has had the best of it.
Notwithstanding all that has been said of Mr. Brown, I
am forced to respect him for his manliness, and it is but
justice to him to confess that when he forms an opinion
he is not afraid to let it be known. If he does force its
adoption upon others, whether they consider it right or

wrong, I don't blame him for the force so much as I despise the others for their weakness. This weakness and timidity converts every great question into an "open question," and every serious difficulty into a juggle. It is the cause of ingenious whereases in resolutions and of long preambles, which pave the way intricately and slyly to compromise results. The Riel amnesty case illustrates my meaning. The idea of one faction feeling bound by the action of another, or of one government being committed to a course because its predecessor had made a move which it condemned, draws too largely upon the credulity of those who know what faction is in this country, to obtain implicit credence. That idea is only equalled by the romance in which the melodramatic patriotism of M. Riel and his friends was shrouded, when credit was given to that very commonplace and cowardly hero for tendering his sword in defence of Manitoba against the Fenians. Why, if there is any person whom an Irish Catholic dislikes thoroughly it is a French Catholic, and *vice versa*, for evidence of which ask any Irish Catholic who has resided in Montreal or Quebec. If Riel had any reason for the action he took at the time of the raid, it was care for his own safety and that of his half-breed companions. But it is not difficult to invent excuses. They are as indigenous in politics as the thistle is in our fields, and the barn-yards of Grit and Tory are bursting with them. While on the Riel subject I may be pardoned for saying that in my opinion the murder of Scott and the amnesty granted to those guilty of putting him to death will stand forever as foul blots on our national escutcheon. Had Scott been killed in action, or in hot blood, or for any reason that would afford the slightest defence on revolutionary or any imaginable ground, other than the gratification of a mere thirst for blood, I would not have a word to say against an amnesty when so many have been induced to petition for it. But as I think that the murder was atrocious in design and intensely cruel in execution, and was wholly objectless, I feel that its perpetrator is one who, out of regard for our common humanity, if nothing else, should be excluded from the pale of society, and driven to seek among savages that mercy he denied to Scott in his hour of agony. With me that murder involves no question of creed or race. It is simply a question whether or not any one shall be allowed to outrage all the instincts of humanity with impunity, and butcher his way to preferment. In all the catalogue of crimes, if there be one which should ostracise its perpetrator from civilization, I think the cold-blooded mangling of Thomas Scott was it. And though no one but myself be found to speak up for one unknown to fame save his death, I do not fear to take my stand on his tenantless grave, and in the name of all that is human, plead for the memory of a friendless Canadian youth, whose only crime was devotion to his Queen and country. Let those who will have their hero in Riel; my poor hero was at least brave and manly. However, politicians think otherwise, so it is idle to waste words in protest now. But I do not believe they do so think, else why the attempt to throw the responsibility of dealing with the matter upon England? There was odium to be incurred, so, as usual, our statesmen sought to have that odium fall upon the authorities

there. It is significant that the organs which are loud-
est against Independence have no word of reprobation
for a system which seeks to weaken the tie between
Canada and England by making the English Government
responsible for everything that is likely to beget dissatisfaction here. Sir John Macdonald did it and Mr. Mackenzie follows suit. Lord Carnarvon seems to have appreciated this, and in a quiet way, which glows with
satire, pooh-poohs the pleas of the Government and tells
them they had better do on 'this side of the Atlantic
whatever has to be done. It is well it should be so.
We want responsibility to be within reach ; if it cannot
be grasped it is useless. Given this responsibility and
we can employ the rest. The people are sound at heart,
and a Pacific Scandal, or any other scandal, will be sum-
marily treated. When a matter of great importance is
brought home to the minds of the people the withes of
party become as tow. This is our encouragement and
the source of our hope. And though it may take time
to develop individuality, to remove the incubus that
forces those possessed of most intelligence to conformity
with those who possess the least, to close the spaces in
which selfishness and sordid motives work, to produce
insensibility to purchased bluster and hireling sycophancy—in fine, to give reason fair-play and honesty breathing room, yet it is pleasant to be able to feel that the
end is capable of attainment, and that in such attainment, even in part, the harvest will be for the benefit of
the many, not merely the few, and that in a higher
type of government, administered on broad, national
principles, the permanence of our Dominion will be
doubly assured.

PARTY *VERSUS* PRINCIPLE.

The Daily Telegraph (Toronto), Aug. 24th, 1867.

IT may now be regarded as quite a natural thing for an uncertain number of people to give their wits leave of absence during the heat and excitement of an election contest. We expect it just as we look for hydrophobia in the dog-days. A lucid interval too protracted would play sad havoc with brains, or the substitute therefor, and cause some heads to fly off like the corks of soda water or ginger-beer bottles. The beneficent provisions of our Constitution, however, furnish opportunities to all so disposed of giving reason a holiday, and it is hardly necessary to say that such are duly improved. Neighbours, long credited with sanity, become suddenly transformed into raving Bacchantes or dancing Dervishes; acquaintances of a genial disposition and quiet nature are seized with a mania for war-paint and feathers; friends, at a given signal, fly at each other's throats and exchange epithets of the most unsavoury character. The demented ones form separate circles, and those of a like mania join hands. Day and night are rendered hideous by their howling. The most untuneful of choruses assail the heavens, while harsh jang-

ling jars on the public ear.   In vain does the quiet-lov-
ing householder vociferate from his window ; in vain his
cry for the police.   The guardian of the public peace
answers that the howls are but the expression of public
opinion, and the discordant medleys an indication of a
healthy party spirit.   Every election time witnesses a
recurrence of these party antics.   But we are glad to say
that there are many whose sense of propriety revolts at
the Saturnalia of purchased inebriety and fury, who do
not relish the language which party puts in the mouths
of its thoughtless dupes, yet have too much at stake to
be indifferent, and too much patriotism to allow mere
noise and glib falsehood to control the destinies of our
common country.   To the latter class we now appeal.
Let the wild man and the sycophant have their fling ; let
them draw tight the lines of party, ay, so tight as to
squeeze out every particle of common sense ; let them
think no thoughts but those that are injected into them,
or speak no words but those furnished cut and dried by
the one or two who rule them ; let them moan and groan,
bellow and cheer as they are ordered ; in fine, let them
give up all the privileges of reasoning beings.   There are
honest, thoughtful men, poor as well as rich, who will not
bow the knee to the Baal of party ; who have sense
enough to do their own thinking and manliness enough
to act on their own convictions of right and wrong, who,
though they may arrive at false conclusions, never do
so blindly or wilfully ; who do not set party before
principle, or place the judgment which God has given
them in subjection to the whim, passion, or pique of their
fellow-man.   To such we would address our words.   This

party-cry which has been raised is both hollow and
hypocritical. Party has been the curse of Canada. It
has placed in the hands of one or two men whips which
they have not hesitated to use to the scarification of the
country. It stayed our progress; it made us the laugh-
ing stock of our neighbours; it ruined our credit abroad,
and destroyed our faith in ourselves; it demoralized our
statesmen and corrupted our people; it wasted valuable
time in idle discussions about general principles, when we
should have devoted all our energies to developing our
resources; and it finally brought our government to a
standstill. Why was the scheme of Confederation accepted with such unanimity? Was it not because it afforded
a prospect of relief from that sickening political squab-
bling which party spirit had carried to the greatest extreme
and opened up a new arena in which statesmanship
might win prizes worth contending for? All our representatives united in supporting it. George Brown and
Sir John Macdonald rivalled each other in prognosticat-
ing the best results in this respect.

A government is in power which embraces the ablest
men of both the old parties. In declared opposition to it
are Mr. Howe and the disunionists of Nova Scotia, the
Rouges of Quebec, and Mr. Brown and Mr. O'Donohoe,
Mr. Halley and Mr. Edgar of Ontario. Mr. Howe opposes
it because it brought about Confederation, the Rouges because they wished to get into power; Mr. Brown because
he deserted his colleagues and has all the hatred of a
deserter; Mr. O'Donohoe because he wants to be made
manager where he is now a mere copyist and clerk; Mr.
Halley because he was not bought off; and Mr. Edgar

because Mr. Brown tells him to do so. The arguments supplied by the *Globe* to the Ontario Opposition are that coalitions are bad, and some members of the government objectionable. Mr. John Macdonald (who was termed a born fool by Mr. Brown) says that he abhors coalitions, but none save a fool would have the effrontery to assert that coalitions are unjustifiable under all circumstances and bad in themselves. Great English statesmen, such as Lords Sidmouth, Grenville, Aberdeen, Palmerston, Sir Wm. Molesworth, Sir James Graham, Mr. Gladstone, and Sidney Herbert were members of coalition governments. Mr. Lincoln did not hesitate to take into his cabinet members of the Democratic party. In our own country such men as the late Mr. Baldwin have frequently ex- pressed an opinion favourable to coalitions where great objects were to be attained. When opposition is offered to the Government merely because it is a coalition, then we say the opposition is hypocrital, more especially so in the case of Mr. Brown, who was a member of it himself. The argument that it is desirable to restore party lines has been disposed of. Mr. Brown is estopped by his own words from urging it, and our experience as a country is directly opposed to it. If Mr. Brown wishes to have a party, and there are persons willing to tie themselves to his coat-tails, he is at liberty to make one. But he must not be allowed to steal the livery of Reform for the pur- pose of concealing the wolfish forms of those who accept his yoke. Mr. Brown ratted. He stole away from the Reform party and then tried to coax them after him. But his efforts have been unsuccessful. If there is such a thing as a Reform party, Mr. Howland, Mr. Macdougall, and Mr. J. S. Macdonald are its leaders. They stuck to the ship.

We attach very little importance to the stories retailed in the *Globe* from day to day about the transactions of a former time. The very same articles were all published by Mr. Brown before he asked Sir John Macdonald to form a coalition and obtained permission to enter a cabinet along with Cartier, Galt, and other corruptionists, swindlers and thieves. No one would be surprised if Mr. Brown tried the same game again under some delusive plea.

The coalition have not yet announced their policy, so there is nothing to oppose. The only issue we see before the electors is whether the Confederation scheme shall be consummated, or Mr. Howe, Mr. Brown, and Mr. Lanctot be allowed to delay it. The machinery of Confederation must be made to work, and none so fit to set it going as the engineers under whose superintendence it was devised. Is Mr. Howe a man to be trusted with the work? He went to England and denounced us as a disloyal and mercenary, factious and poverty-stricken people. He sneered at our efforts to lift ourselves from obscurity, abused our public men, and held us up to the derision of the mother country. He satirized our backwoods manners, and cast mean reflections upon the refinment of our wives and daughters. Though a colonist himself, he outraged every instinct of humanity in an endeavour to gain pre-eminence through the belittling of his kindred, his countrymen, his home, Is he the colleague whom Mr. Brown wishes to have? Is he the man we of this province desire as our ruler?

And now, when in spite of discouragements, in spite of obstacles seemingly insuperable, in spite of internal selfishness and external menace, we have got so far in the good work of union, we are asked to halt, to fight the old battles over again, to disregard the wants of the country, to overlook practical legislation, and commence a senseless wrangling over party politics. In the past we have had too much politics; in the future we want more work. Talk may be good, but work is better. Let the elector who is trying to see clearly what his duty is, ponder over what we have said, and we are convinced that unless he is a mere party hack, he will come to the conclusion that country should be placed before party, that good measures for developing our agricultural, manufacturing, and mineral resources are to be preferred to all the speeches of disappointed politicians, and that the future of our country demands united and energetic action at this juncture of affairs.

THE CANADIAN CONFEDERACY.*

HE probable fate of the British North American colonies has, for many years, afforded wide scope for speculation. Both in this country and in America the chances have been weighed as passing events offer themselves for analysis. It has been regarded from various points of view; the result being, conclusions as widely different as such topics of discussion usually lead to. Argument resting on a speculative basis is always unsteady, and kaleidoscopic glances at the present yield very unsatisfactory data from which to decipher the future. Hence it is that America and American affairs have so frequently belied prophecy. The conjectures evoked by the dealings between England and her North American colonies have in many instances proved erroneous, and we are not now so liable to be led astray by the oracular utterances of nervousness and timidity. We were assured that Canada was incapable of self-control, but we find that political strife carried to the extreme has not been able to weaken the springs of government, or to disregard the promptings of patriotism. Petty recriminations and jealousies, which formerly found vent in the Colonial Office, have been smothered where their origin could be soonest detected and their object most

* From the *Westminster Review*, April, 1865.

easily frustrated. The consequence of transferring responsibility from the shoulders of the Imperial Government to those of the colonists themselves, is that the
shafts of temper no longer spend their force on an imperial target, while a spirit of loyalty and affection has
taken the place of an ungracious allegiance. It has also
been asserted that the democratic tendencies of these
American colonies would have the effect of weakening if
not terminating the relations between them and the
mother country ; that the grant of freedom from imperial dictation naturally handed over to republicanism the
keys of a British stronghold. Neither has this proved
true, although the anticipation harmonizes well with the
expressed wishes of the United States. So long ago as
1775, when delegates from the American States assembled in convention at Philadelphia to agree upon the
terms of an union, they evidently accepted as a foregone
conclusion the immediate entrance of Canada, at least,
into the federal compact, for Section XI. of their Articles of Agreement provided that " Canada, acceding to
the confederation and joining in the measures of the
United States, shall be admitted into and be entitled to
the advantages of the Union." Every inducement to revolt was held out to all the British provinces ; but
neither open temptation nor secret intrigue was sufficiently powerful to allure them from their allegiance. Lower
Canada was appealed to in terms that recognized its peculiar position as regards race, language, religion and
laws, and included a guarantee for their security and
permanence. But the French inhabitants, besides having
the recollection of past wrongs to prompt a rejection,
were moved by a deep-rooted antipathy to republican-

ism to meet with disdain overtures thus insidiously made to them. In after years the employment of force had as little effect in changing the determination of these stubborn colonists to remain a portion of the empire: and the several provinces not only fought nobly against the common enemy, but even sent assistance to the more sorely pressed. Notwithstanding this, it has been an article of political faith with American statesmen and politicians that the "manifest destiny" of their republic would, in its own good time, lead to the absorption of some, if not all, of the adjacent British provinces. To embrace these is their traditionary policy, having in its list of founders and supporters such names as Washington, Franklin, Monroe, and Seward. Mr. Seward's views pointed to a peaceable rather than a forcible annexation; and both in England and in British America the idea has been entertained that Canada, New Brunswick, and Nova Scotia, but more especially the first-named, must sooner or later cast in their lot with the powerful nation at their side, impelled by sheer force of political attraction. Nor is this theory incapable of support, though formerly the reasons in its favour were much more numerous than they now are. A glance at the position occupied by Canada a few years ago will be found to justify in some degree the Montreal annexation movement of 1849. It was a dependency shut in from the seaboard for five months of the year, at an enormous distance from the imperial metropolis; separated from those of kindred sympathies, and acknowledging a like allegiance, by an almost untraversable tract of country; exposed to attack at every point along a frontier of a thousand miles; gazing at the prosperity of a nation which held out every inducement to unite with it; without manufactures, coal or capital, yet witnessing a stream of British wealth pouring into the lap of its rival; thinly populated, and outbid in attracting emigration; with the hope of union between itself and the other British colonies uncertain, although having all the elements of prosperity ready to be combined, but suffering them, from various causes, to lie unimproved and unprofitable. Taking every circumstance into consideration, it cannot be denied that the prospects of a long continued existence of such a dependency as a separate and distinct political organism were dim and dubious. The maritime provinces had not such influences to contend against; but the temptations brought to bear upon Canada, and her successful resistance to them, naturally beget surprise at the nature of the causes to which she owed her preservation from a loss of identity in the nation at her side. It is unnecessary, however, for present purposes to do more than notice the fact, as it serves to show the bent of her inclination. Changed times have suggested new fields for debate, and prophecy has been driven to seek out new channels. A rapid advance in material prosperity has brought with it considerations left out in previous forecasts; while, on the other hand, the American Republic presents to its admirers fewer attractions than formerly. The effect is seen in the almost total obliteration of annexation sentiment in the colonies, and in the strength and encouragement afforded to those in England who looked forward to the establishment of a British nationality in America that would not only rival the great republic, but would prove a faithful ally to the mother land. When we yielded to these colonies the right of self-government, we gave up the right to dictate, whether we reserved the privilege of guiding or not. This abandonment of control carried with it, said some, the last link in the chain that bound our British American colonies to the empire; but this hasty assertion has been thus far falsified. Confident in their capacity for self-government, we committed their fortunes to their own keeping, as a faithful guardian unburdens himself of his trust on the attainment of majority by his ward. Had we conceived that this transfer involved a mere change of masters, we should have hesitated to sacrifice our interests to those of a foreign power. But faith in their future was no less strong with our statesmen than it was in the colonists themselves. That self-reliance, that innate vigor, which defies misfortune and begets self-confidence, is a characteristic of our race, and, when grafted in other lands, reproduces its inherent qualities with the characteristics of the parent stock. We had confidence in our kindred and in the virtue of our institutions; and a colonial policy based upon this has proved successful, and in its success its wisdom. A complex relationship has been begotten, but the machinery has worked tolerably well. The evidences of stability exhibited by these self-governed colonies, the variety of resources at their command, and the vast progress they have made in utilizing the advantages placed by nature within their reach, have not been lost sight of by that school of politicians which regards the relations between us and the states dependent but in name as presenting some unsatisfactory features. Nor

G

has the change in circumstances been passed over heedlessly by the colonists themselves. They, too, have begun
to reflect on the chances of the future. Everlasting
youth is denied to nations as well as to individuals, and
impulses from within combine with influences from without to urge a consideration of the best means for ensuring a lusty manhood. It is with no little pride, therefore, that we see them enter upon the discussion of a
subject of such vital importance as a confederation
among themselves with calmness and deliberation indicat-
ing a knowledge of the responsibility devolving upon
them, and a determination to probe to the bottom the
secret of national greatness. It is a complete vindication
of our modern policy in permitting them to think and act
for themselves. It is of importance, therefore, to know
what they propose to do, the basis of the contemplated
changes, and their effect. To arrive at a proper understanding, it is necessary to go back a little in their
history.

It must not be supposed that the scheme of confederation is the offspring of fear. Its origin can be traced
much further back than the civil war in the United
States, however much a shock so terrible may have contributed to its maturity; nor can colonial emancipators,
should their anticipations be realized, lay claim to its in-
ception, however entitled to the credit of supplying a
reason for its adoption.

It is stated that as early as 1810 a union of all the
British American provinces was suggested by one of the
colonists, Mr. Uniacke, of Nova Scotia, and at various
times afterwards the attention of the imperial authorities

was directed to the subject by leading colonial politicians. Chief-Justice Sewell, of Quebec, in 1814 laid before the late Duke of Kent a comprehensive plan, which met with the approval of His Royal Highness. In 1827, resolutions were introduced into the Legislative Assembly of Upper Canada, directed more especially to a union of the two provinces of Upper and Lower Canada; but proposing, as an alternative, "what would be more politic, wise, and generally advantageous,—viz., a union of the whole four provinces of North America under a vice-royalty, with a facsimile of that great and glorious fabric—the best monument of human wisdom—the British Constitution."

Lord Durham, in his report on the affairs of British North America (1839), discusses the subject at considerable length, anticipating nearly all the arguments that can now be urged in its favour. In 1854, resolutions were brought forward in the Nova Scotia Legislature which indicated a strong desire to promote a closer connexion of the different provinces; and in 1857 the subject was pressed upon Mr. Labouchere, then Secretary of State for the Colonies, by delegates from that province; but he felt disposed to leave it to the colonists themselves to take action in the matter. In 1858, the Canadian Government announced as part of their policy that the expediency of a federal union of the British North-American provinces would be anxiously considered, and that communications would be entered into with the other provinces and the Imperial Government to secure adhesion to the project. In accordance with this announcement, delegates were sent from Canada, and the sanction of the Imperial Government was asked to the scheme; but the hesitation exhibited by the other provinces rendered the effort thus made fruitless. In 1861, the government of Nova Scotia made the next move, and in 1863 both Houses of the Nova Scotia Legislature passed unanimously resolutions authorizing the appointment of delegates to confer upon that subject with delegates from the other maritime provinces. Similar resolutions were adopted in the Parliaments of New Brunswick and Prince Edward Island. A meeting of delegates was accordingly called to sit at Charlotte Town, Prince Edward Island, in September of 1864.

Meanwhile, events in Canada were rapidly tending to render some change in its political condition an absolute necessity. One government after another was forced to confess itself unable to control Parliament; and resignation followed resignation, and election succeeded election, with no other effect than to increase the embarrassment. The result was that sectional majorities, firmly united, impeded legislation, and assailed each other with every weapon that strong sectional differences place at the disposal of political factions. Lower Canadian representatives united to resist the demands of their compeers from the Upper Province, and Upper Canadian members were as resolute in enforcing what they considered to be just claims. In fact, Upper and Lower Canada were arrayed against each other, each determined not to yield an inch of ground. This state of things, it was evident, could not long continue without leading to very serious results. The nature of the questions on which the two were divided admitted of no immediate satisfactory compromise, considering the relative position of the disputants. Upper Canadian members alleged that the population of their section of the province exceeded that of the other by 400,000 ; and as each had an equality of representation, the result was the practical disenfranchisement of these 400,000. It was also contended that the proportion of taxation raised by the respective sections showed a large excess in favour of Upper Canada, as that portion paid two-thirds of the taxation of the country, while the relative expenditure exhibited a gross injustice. In answer to this, Lower Canadians contended that, at the time of the union of the provinces, their section had a majority of 175,000 ; and it was not till 1850 that the scale was turned against them, by reason of a large immigration; and that they (comparatively rich) had borne the heavier part of the burden of a debt contracted by the Upper Province, which, at the time, was staggering under the load; that any increase in the representation in Parliament would naturally place them (being a minority) at the mercy of a people dissimilar in race, character, religion, language, and laws. This quarrel culminated on the floor of Parliament, as we have already mentioned, in arraying sections against each other; the one bold in pressing for increased representation, and the other defiant in resisting it. The union effected between the provinces of Upper and Lower Canada in 1840 was, after all, but a nominal one ; each section preserved its identity, and the line between them remained in all its distinctness. The government has been administered by a ministry made up of an equal number from both sections, with, in most instances, a distinct staff of crown officers. It was, of course, to be expected that local politicians would keep alive sectional prejudices with such material as they had to work upon. Each half of the provincial cabinet has been expected to command the support of a majority from the section it represented, so that a ministry having a majority of the whole Houses of Parliament would be compelled to disband by reason of not having a majority within a majority. This policy could have but one effect, and it may be seen that the secret of frequent political crises lies, therefore, on the surface of Canadian politics. No government could be expected to stand out for any great length of time against a vigilant opposition, with so many conflicting interests to appease as the circumstances and extent of the country created. Party spirit loses none of its violence by reason of the smallness of the community in which it is developed; and in its choice of weapons misses no advantage through courtesy. The check given to public business brought both political parties to their senses; and returning reason suggested the necessity for a remedy by which responsible government would be saved from degenerating into a series of faction fights. It was apparent that constitutional difficulties lay at the bottom of this sectional strife. Both parties accepted the omen; the political leaders avowed their willingness to throw aside party ties and even personal feeling; and a coalition was formed pledged to co-operate in searching out a practical remedy for the evils which had become intolerable. The result is embodied in the following memorandum, which expressed the policy of the coalition government :—

" The Government are prepared to pledge themselves to bring in a measure, next session, for the purpose of removing existing difficulties, by introducing the federal principle into Canada coupled with such provisions as will permit the Maritime Provinces and the North-West Territory to be incorporated with the same system of government ; and the Government will seek, by sending representatives to the Lower Provinces and to England, to secure the assent of those interests that are beyond the control of our Legislature, to be united under a general Legislature based upon the federal system."*

This coalition of parties being accepted as a guarantee for the cessation of that species of political contention which had proved a source of constant annoyance and irritation, met with the unanimous approbation of both Houses of Parliament, and gave satisfaction to the people and press of the country ; while the policy announced afforded a gleam of hope to those who had begun to despair of an adjustment of difficulties hitherto seemingly incapable of settlement. After the prorogation of the Canadian Parliament, an invitation was extended by the Chamber of Commerce of St. John, New Brunswick, to the members of the Canadian Legislature, to pay a visit to the Maritime Provinces. This was accepted by a large number of Canadians, and the principal citizens of New Brunswick and Nova Scotia gave a hearty welcome to their fellow colonists. Their fraternal meetings went far to pave the way for an union, as public attention was at once turned towards the mutual advantage to be gained by a closer connexion. Such an incident may, at first glance, seem of little importance ; but when we consider

* Statement by Hon. J. A. Macdonald in Canadian House of Assembly. June 21, 1864.

that up to this time public opinion had not kept pace
with the dreams of the colonial statesmen (although individuals in all the provinces had agreed on what ought
to be done rather than on what could be done), we are
inclined to give it due weight. Shortly afterwards, the
convention appointed to consider the subject of an union
of the Maritime Provinces, met at Charlottetown, Prince
Edward Island; and members of the Canadian Government attended and proposed to merge in the higher plan
of a confederation of all the provinces,—that of a legislative union among the Maritime Provinces. The subject
was discussed, and such progress made that it was thought
desirable by the Conference that the subject should be
resumed in an official manner under the authority of the
governments of the several provinces.* The Governor-
General of Canada communicated to the Secretary of State
for the Colonies the suggestions of the Conference, stating in his despatch that "the desire for a closer union
amongst the colonies than has hitherto existed appears to
be generally felt both in Canada and the Lower Provinces;" and further, "it appears to me that the mode
of proceeding suggested is the only one in which the
views entertained by the leading politicians of the British
North American colonies on this important subject can
be brought intelligibly and in a practical form before
your attention." In reply, Mr. Cardwell merely expressed
his approval of the course taken in the matter. Official
delegates were appointed to represent each province, with
the exception of Newfoundland. That province, however,

---

* Report of Committee of Executive Council of Canada, Sept. 23, 1864.

was represented by some of its leading statesmen. The Conference met at Quebec, and formally entered upon the discussion of the subject.

From the foregoing it will be observed that the idea of a possible federation has never been extinct in any of the provinces, although it has taken Rip Van Winkle slumbers. Until lately it had not been made a party question, nor had its discussion enlisted any large number of persons. Now, however, it has assumed the proportions of a public question, and invites inquiry into its merits or demerits. Before reviewing the conclusions arrived at by the Conference, it may be as well to take a rapid survey of the country embraced by the confederation scheme, so that we may be enabled to judge of its probable success.

Public attention has but seldom been directed to the capabilities and resources of the British American provinces as a whole : even among the colonists themselves has this been the case, and to such a degree that their knowledge of each other, not to mention the little importance they attach to their united value, has been as slight as our acquaintance with them has been superficial. They have had a strange impression of each other, and until lately, when they began to take stock, the general public had no idea that the provinces would unitedly possess all the elements necessary to constitute a powerful nation. No inducements were offered to render the acquisition of correct information of any practical service ; so that while individuals regarded as visionaries bestowed time and labour in laying a basis for their schemes of future action, the mass of the communities paid little attention to their facts, and gave themselves no trouble about their theories.

Each province has been so taken up with its own needs and the working out of its own projects, that greater interests have been kept in the background. But events have forced them to take thought for the future as well as to provide for the necessities of the present, and in setting out they naturally compare themselves with others.

The British possessions on the American continent embrace a territory nearly equal to that of the United States. It is difficult to give with accuracy the area under British rule, as that portion of the continent is but partially surveyed, and boundaries are not yet clearly defined, but an estimate sufficient for practical purposes has been formed. The latest calculation has this result:

	Square miles.
Canada	331,282
Newfoundland	40,200
New Brunswick	27,105
Nova Scotia	18,660
Prince Edward Island	2,131
	419,378

If we add to this the probable area of the remainder—say, British Columbia 213,500, Vancouver Island 16,000, and the Hudson Bay Territory 1,570,500,—the sum total will show 2,218,641 square miles against 2,963,666, which is the area of the great American Republic given in the Report for 1853 of the American Topographical Bureau. A very large portion of this immense tract of country on both sides of the line is of course incapable of cultivation, but the proportion really valuable even for agricultural purposes is very great. Confining ourselves to the North-American provinces likely to be included in the proposed confederation at once, we find, according to the statement of the Hon. George Brown, made at Halifax on Sept. 12, 1864, and alleged to be based upon the statistics of 1861, that the amount of land held by private individuals in the various provinces, with the number of acres under cultivation, stand respectively as follows—

	Held.		Cultivated.
Upper Canada	17,708,232	...	6,051,619
Lower Canada	13,680,000	...	4,804,235
Nova Scotia	5,748,893	..	1,028,032
New Brunswick	6,636,329	...	835,108
Newfoundland	100,000	...	41,108
Prince Edward Island	1,365,400	...	368,127
	45,238,854		13,128,229

Without referring to the agricultural produce of the provinces, which may be always looked to as the basis of their prosperity, and which now yields about 150,-000,000 dollars annually, we shall now glance at other features which, though less important at present, yet afford for consideration an inviting aspect. Besides a fertile soil and magnificent forests, the provinces possess inexhaustible mineral resources, such as are accessories to civilization, and material attractions to enterprise and skill. In Nova Scotia, gold, iron, coal, and copper are found in abundance. The quantity of coal at present raised is half a million of tons per annum. Four years ago gold was discovered, and now 151 mines are being worked, yielding in the way of revenues and royalties 20,000 dollars annually. New Brunswick, in common with Nova Scotia, has gold, iron, and extensive coal deposits, extending over seven millions of acres. Newfoundland has a coal formation of 1000 to 1500 feet in thickness; but it has not been worked, owing to other more profitable employments absorbing the attention of the inhabitants. As Canada has no coal, though abundance of iron ore and copper, it will be seen what an important bearing the possibility of obtaining supplies from the Lower Provinces may have in other years. Gold has been found in Canada, but thus far the yield is insignificant. Throughout the mineral regions of Canada, forest trees exist in sufficient abundance to render the absence of coal for smelting purposes less felt than it otherwise would be. But the time will come when, wood being no longer at the disposal of the miner, coal will have to be resorted to. The profusion of iron ore in Canada, awaiting the magic touch of the capitalist to add to the country's riches, is wonderful; and the copper mines in both the Upper and Lower Provinces have already given such evidences of productiveness as to justify the expressed opinion as to their national value.

Apart from these agricultural and mineral resources, there exists a guarantee for solid prosperity in the exhaustless fisheries that lie at the very threshold of the proposed Confederacy. Their value cannot be over-estimated, and the many times they have been the subject of diplomatic contest shows that their importance has been in some degree appreciated. For several centuries the governments of various countries have regarded them with envious eye. France has ever shown herself eager to push her interests in this quarter, and placing a proper estimate on their commercial and political importance, has lavished large sums on what she regarded as an investment producing an adequate money return as well as a nursery for her seamen.* It was a maxim with the French Government that the North-American fisheries were of more national value in regard to navigation and power than the gold mines of Mexico could have been if the latter were possessed by France. The number of men now employed by her in these fishing stations is about 11,500, and for years large bounties have been paid to encourage her seamen to engage in the occupation of fishing. The return from the French fisheries cannot be less than 3,000,000 dollars a year. On January 14, 1857, the French Government obtained from England certain concessions relative to fishery rights on the coast of Newfoundland, but the alarm created in the Maritime Provinces by what they looked upon as inflicting injury upon their interests, and the refusal of Newfoundland to accede to the terms of the treaty prevented it from taking effect. Nor are the United States wanting in appreciation of the benefits to be derived from a prosecution of this branch of trade. President Pierce, in his Message to Congress (Dec. 1862), in alluding to the Reciprocity Treaty, said : " The treaty between the United States and Great Britain of 5th June, 1854, which went into effective operation in 1855, put an end to causes of irritation between the two countries by securing to the United States the right of fishing on the coast of the British North-American Pro-

---

* See the Report by M. Ancet for 1851, and that by M. Coste for 1861.

vinces with advantages equal to those enjoyed by British
subjects.   Besides the signal benefits of this treaty to a
large class of our citizens in a pursuit connected in no
inconsiderable degree with our national prosperity and
strength, it has had a favourable effect, &c."   The
amount expended in bounties now averages 300,000 dollars annually, and the return is estimated at about eight
and a half millions of dollars.   The advantage of position enjoyed by the Maritime Provinces naturally at-
tracts capital and enterprise from other pursuits to profit
by an employment so lucrative as that placed by nature
within their very grasp.   They see with chagrin the
treasures of the deep snatched from before their eyes,
and going to the enrichment of foreigners, while the
apathy of their fellow-colonists living inland prevents a
just share being appropriated by those who should profit
most by them.   Without a system of bounties (except
as regards Canada) the value of fish, fish-oil, and seal-
skins exported from these provinces (independently of
what was consumed in domestic use) is thus given—

Nova Scotia	.	.	.	$2,335,104
New Brunswick (1862)		.	.	303,487
Newfoundland (1862) .		.	.	3,760,010
Prince Edward Island*		.	.	
Canada (1862)	.	.	.	703,896

We have not the returns necessary to found an accurate statement of the aggregate value of these fisheries,

---

*We regret to be unable to obtain in time for publication in this article
the statement of the value of fish, etc., exported from Prince Edward
Island.

but competent authorities have suggested 20,000,000 dollars as falling short of the actual yield.

Possessing 5,000 miles of sea-coast, the British North American provinces when consolidated into one power would possess not only all the materials necessary for constructing and equipping ships of war, but also bands of skilful and hardy seamen wherewith to man a powerful fleet. Already their united commercial marine shows an amount of tonnage that would entitle a Confederacy such as is proposed to take high rank as a maritime power. The following table shows the tonnage required for the accommodation of trade :—

	Inwards.	Outwards.	Total.
Nova Scotia (1863)	712,939..	719,915..	1,432,954
New Brunswick	659,258..	727,722..	1,386,980
Prince Edward Island (1861) .	79,580..	87,518..	167,098
Newfoundland (1861). . . .	696,763..	695,582..	1,392,345
Canada (1863)	4,580,010..	4,460,327..	9,040,337
	6,728,550	6,691,064	13,419,614

The tonnage employed by Canada on the inland lakes is stated to be 6,907,000 tons, but this includes many coasting vessels, between whose arrival and departure a very short interval elapses, so that a very great deduction must be made to express correctly the actual tonnage. But the sea-going tonnage of Canada amounts to 2,133,000 tons. The opportunities for commerce are such as to indicate the natural increase of the colonial marine. The facilities for ship-building turn the attention of a large number not only to the supply of the home demand, but also to competition in foreign markets for the sale of vessels.

In 1832 the tonnage of vessels built in British America amounted to only 33,776 tons; in 1863 the number of vessels built was 645, with a capacity of 219,763 tons,[*] and representing an export value of 9,000,000 dollars. The number of sailors and fishermen of these colonies, as shown by the last census returns, is 69,256.

The total population of the united colonies cannot be said to indicate great strength, considering the vast region over which it is spread; it must, however, be regarded as a respectable nucleus of a nationality which the varied resources of the country will in time fill up and extend by attracting immigration. In five years Nova Scotia has doubled her population, while Canada has increased from 1,147,349 in 1842 to 2,507,657 in 1861; Upper Canada presenting the most rapid increase, as in 1842 her population numbered 486,055, and in 1861, 1,396,091. The population of the six provinces is represented by the census of 1861 to be thus distributed:— Upper Canada, 1,396,091; Lower Canada, 1,111,566; Nova Scotia, 330,857; New Brunswick, 252,047; Newfoundland (1863), 124,288; Prince Edward Island, 80,857 : total, 3,295,706. Adding to this the increase from every source since 1861, and the numbers necessarily omitted, the whole population may be assumed to be nearly 4,000,000 of souls. If we place this aggregate in comparison with the population of European countries ranking as substantial powers—for instance, Portugal, 3,570,000; Holland, 3,500,000; Denmark, 2,480,000; Greece, 1,150,000—we are enabled to form a pretty fair

*Speech of Finance Minister of Canada, February 7th, 1865.

idea of the position a British confederacy may ere long hold among the nations of the earth. The following tabulated statement shows the fighting material available for defensive purposes :—

Upper Canada, from	20 to 30	..	128,740
	30 to 40	..	84,178
	40 to 50	..	59,660
	50 to 60	..	36,377—308,955
Lower Canada, from	20 to 30	..	93,302
	30 to 40		59,507
	40 to 50	..	42,628
	50 to 60	..	30,129—225,620
Nova Scotia, from	20 to 60	..	— 67,367
New Brunswick, from	21 to 40	..	33,574
	40 to 50	..	10,739
	50 to 60	..	7,312— 51,625
Newfoundland, from	20 to 60	..	— 25,532
Prince Edward Island, from	20 to 45	..	11,144
	45 to 60	..	3,675— 14,819
Total males from	20 to 60	..	693,918

The ebb and flow of the tide of population in a new country such as America presents curious results. While the population is being augmented from without, localities and sections of country suffer from the constant drain made upon them by the attractions of older or more inviting parts of the continent. The young Canadian or Nova Scotian, seduced by the prospects of an enlarged scope for ambition or the hope of acquiring a fortune more rapidly than he could do at home, deserts his native land to push his way into the adjoining States or the ex-

H

treme west of the continent. Even the French Canadians, noted for their attachment to their native soil, become restive, and are found bold enough to seek new homes among a people whom they have been taught to regard as hostile to all they hold sacred. The number of British colonists now residing in the United States is very great. It is said that there are 20,000 Canadians alone in the Federal army. What has contributed to this self-expatriation has undoubtedly been the want of intercourse between colonies which offer every inducement to industry. Instead of an interchange of floating population, the current has gone in a foreign direction, and thousands of young men have not only been lost to the colonies, but have gone to the building up of their rivals. As districts now scarcely rescued from native wildness become more closely settled, and intervening tracts that serve as so many barriers to communication are pierced by advancing civilization, communities now almost strangers to each other will feel the uniting influences of trade, and present to the colonial youth a greater diversity of pursuits than the limited means and distracted energies of each province have been able to open up.

Notwithstanding the disadvantages incident to divided counsels and sectional legislation, the provinces have advanced very rapidly in material wealth. Small markets have stunted their manufactures, but their great staples have enabled them to grasp and retain a fast hold on international trade. Their exports and imports already exceed those of the United States in 1821. The returns of 1863 are presented in one view in the following table :—

	Imports.	Exports.	Total.
Canada	$45,964,493 ..	$41,831,532 ..	$87,796,025
New Brunswick . .	7,764,824 ..	8,964,784 ..	16,729,608
Nova Scotia . . .	10,201,391 ..	8,420,968 ..	18,622,359
Prince Edward Island	1,428,028 ..	1,627,540 ..	3,055,568
Newfoundland . .	5,242,720 ..	6,002,312 ..	11,245,032
	$70,601,456	$66,847,136	$137,448,592

While this trade in the aggregate is large, the part of it
strictly intercolonial bears but a small proportion to that
carried on with foreign countries. In 1863 the total imports by the St. Lawrence from the British North American colonies to Canada amounted to $568,806, and the
exports of Canada to the other colonies to $992,738.
This low state of intercolonial trade is attributable to the
hostile tariffs put in force by each province, amounting
in effect to the exclusion of each other's products. Free
trade between them will no doubt remedy the evil to a
great extent. In the three years preceding the Reciprocity Treaty, the exports of the United States to these
provinces were $48,216,518, and the imports $22,588,577.
During the ten years in which the treaty has been in
operation, from 1854 to 1863, the expansion has been
unexampled, showing an aggregate of exports to the
value of $256,350,931, and of imports to the value of
$200,399,786.* It is very natural for the colonists to
argue that if reciprocity between them and the United
States lent such an impetus to trade, reciprocity between
all the provinces would likewise cause an increase in

---

* Senator Sumner—Speech on the Reciprocity Treaty in Congress, Jan.
11, 1865.

their trade with each other. A large proportion of the goods which the maritime provinces now buy in the States could be supplied by Canada, and the competition would not be with the productions of Great Britain, but with those of the States.* The imports of all kinds of agricultural produce in New Brunswick amounted in one year to $2,060,702, of which Canada supplied only $177,328. Most of the flour is of Canada growth and manufacture, and instead of its being procured from Portland in the United States it could be laid down at the head of the St. John River in New Brunswick as cheaply as it is carried to Portland. The New Brunswick Comptroller of Customs, in his report for 1863, says : " If New Brunswick were connected with Montreal and Quebec by direct railway communication through British territory, our imports from the States would decrease immediately, as much of our flour and other supplies could come direct from Canada." The same might be said of the other provinces. The subject of intercolonial reciprocity has been considered by the colonists, and various schemes have been suggested to change a state of things which all looked upon as anomalous, but which, being beset with difficulties, offered little prospect of a satisfactory or immediate improvement. In 1862 the Legislature of Nova Scotia passed resolutions empowering the Government to negotiate with the neighbouring provinces for an interchange of articles duty free. The Finance Minister of Canada gave his attention to the proposition, and re-

---

* Report of Canadian Finance Minister on Intercolonial Reciprocity, 1862.

ported to his colleagues the result of his examination.
He said :—

"If a complete customs union could be formed between the provinces under which they could interchange, without restriction, all
goods the produce and manufacture of whatever country, it would
have a beneficial effect. But as, to carry such a union conveniently
into effect, greater uniformity in the tariffs of the colonies must be
secured, which would be almost impracticable under their present
condition, the undersigned contents himself with recommending
that, in answer to the despatch of the Nova Scotia Government, a
proposal be made for the reciprocal free admission of all articles the
growth, produce, and manufacture of Nova Scotia and any other
province becoming a party to the agreement that may be founded
on this proposal."

The delegates from the provinces of Canada, Nova Scotia,
and New Brunswick, who met to consider the subject,
came to the conclusion that the free interchange of goods
and uniformity of tariff were indispensable consequences
of the construction of the intercolonial railway, and that
the diminution of the revenues of the respective provinces, from various causes, did not warrant the adoption
of measures to carry the principle into effect.

The necessity for a line of railway between Canada and
the Lower Provinces has been apparent for years past,
and the project has occupied the attention of the imperial
as well as the colonial authorities. The trade of Canada
is dependent, in a great degree, upon the temper and feelings of the United States. For five months in the year
exit by the St. Lawrence is completely cut off, and during this period Portland is the Canadian seaport. Should
the Portland section of the Grand Trunk Railway be
closed at any time, all communication with Europe must

be carried on by the overland route to Halifax, and
Canada would be forced to resort to the old system of
importation by way of the St. Lawrence during the season
of open navigation.   The repeal of the Reciprocity Treaty
and the abolition of the bonding system will compel
Canada to find other outlets than those now available,
and will force her to seek relief from a virtual blockade
by connecting herself with the other colonies.   For defensive purposes the road may also be of advantage, in
enabling masses of troops to pass rapidly from province
to province.   However, as matters now stand, it is the
only possible way of forestalling the consequences of complete isolation.   The importance of the undertaking has
never been questioned.

Lord Durham, in the report to which we have already
referred, said—" The completion of any satisfactory communication between Halifax and Quebec would in fact
produce relations between these provinces that would
render a general union absolutely necessary."   In 1843
the Imperial Government caused a survey to be made
with reference to a military road, and in 1848 Major
Robinson and Captain Henderson reported as to the fitness for rail purposes of the proposed route.   In a correspondence between Lord Elgin and Earl Grey in 1848,
the former insisted strongly on the advantages likely to
accrue from the construction of the line ; among others,
that it would " tend to unite the provinces to one another
and to the mother country, and to inspire them with that
consciousness of their own strength and of the value of
the connexion with Great Britain, which is their best
security against aggression."   The Legislatures of Canada,

New Brunswick, and Nova Scotia passed acts for the promotion of the undertaking. In 1851, Lord Derby, in the House of Lords, expressed himself in favour of the construction of the line; and in 1852 Sir John Pakington, in a despatch to Lord Elgin, gave expression to the views of the Imperial Government, declaring their intention to fulfil the just expectations held out by their predecessors. In a despatch from the Duke of Newcastle, dated April 12, 1862, a proposal was made, couched in the following terms :—

" Anxious, however, to promote as far as they can the important object of completing the great line of railway communication on British ground between the Atlantic and the westernmost parts of Canada, and to assist the provinces in a scheme which would so materially promote their interests, her Majesty's Government are willing to offer to the Provincial Governments an imperial guarantee of interest towards enabling them to raise by public loan, if they should desire it, at a moderate rate, the requisite funds for constructing the railway. . . . The nature and extent of such guarantee must be determined by the particulars of any scheme which the Provincial Governments may be disposed to found on the present proposal, and on the kind of security they would offer."

In September, 1862, delegates duly appointed by the provinces met at Quebec to consider the proposal, and a memorandum of agreement was drawn up. Owing to a subsequent dissatisfaction with some of the conditions precedent proposed by the Imperial Government, the effort proved abortive. The objections to the construction of the line have been the probable immediate loss connected with it as a commercial speculation, owing to the insufficiency of paying freights, the difficulty of keeping it in running order in winter, and its uselessness for military purposes, owing to its proximity to the frontier. In its favour the argument rests on a national, military, and commercial basis; that it furnishes the surest means of bringing about a confederation, that it will enable troops to be moved rapidly across British territory, and facilitate the concentration of masses of men, and that it will counterbalance to a certain extent the pressure of the United States on Canada by affording another method by which the foreign mails can be carried, and access to the seaboard obtained for Canadian products and manufactures; besides effecting a saving of time in the transmission of European and American correspondence. The length of railway to be built is estimated at 350 miles;* this, however, may be under the mark. When this line is constructed there will be a complete railway connection from Halifax on the Atlantic to the shores of Lake Huron.

Thus far the energies of the different provinces have been directed to schemes of internal improvement, promoting facility of internal communication, and every effort has been put forth to secure the vast trade of the West, whose natural channel is the St. Lawrence. Costly though the struggle has proved, yet it is not fruitless. Every mile of railway has paid for itself tenfold in opening up the country and increasing the value of property, and the magnificent canal system has overcome the natural obstacles by which navigation was impeded and commerce forced into other and foreign channels. The

---

* Despatch of Duke of Newcastle, April 12th, 1862.

benefits conferred will not be confined to one province, but must be shared with all to a greater or less extent, from their very nature. To sustain and extend the public works already in existence, and to call others into being that will act as feeders to them, can only be done efficiently, where the aim is a common prosperity, by unity of action and a clubbing of resources It will be found that the Canadian Confederacy will set out with a respectable income. Its financial standing may be judged of from the following statement of liabilities, revenue, and expenditures :—

1863.	Debt.	Receipts.	Payments.
Canada.................	$67,263,995..	$14,382,508..	$14,909,182
New Brunswick..........	5 778,000..	894,836..	884,613
Nova Scotia (about).......	5,000,000..	1,185,629..	1,072,274
Newfoundland...........	946,000..	480,000..	479,420
Prince Edward Island....	240,673..	197,384..	171,718
	$79,228,668	$17,140,357	$17,517,207

Summing up the resources of the provinces about to assume the attitude of a distinct power, we find that they possess every element that enters into the formation of a nationality which will, if properly guided, stand the test of time.

We are thus enabled to see at a glance the magnitude of the interests to be dealt with by the delegates appointed to the Quebec Conference, and we can imagine the difficulties that presented themselves at every step in their negotiations, while striving to reconcile the prejudices of localities hitherto having complete control over their own affairs. The necessity for securing differ-

ent races against mutual aggression, and protecting religious views from an intolerance already busy in sowing
seeds of discord, involved problems not easy of solution.
Had there been any inclination to trifle with the main
object of their meeting, or a disposition to throw
obstacles in the way of its attainment, the result of the
convention would have extinguished all hope of a British
American confederation for years to come, as well as
suggested grave doubts as to the future peace and welfare
of colonies so situated as the British North-American
colonies are. But great responsibilities outweighed nar·
row-minded views, and mutual concession enabled the
delegates to lay down a substantial basis for a consolidated government. The scheme is outlined with prudent
forethought, and in detail evinces the care of practical
statesmanship. As a whole it is acceptable, taking it for
granted that it is the best that could be arrived at. Its
authors tell us that they were anxious to follow, as far as
circumstances would permit, the model of the British
Constitution. How far circumstances controlled their
desires, an examination of the prominent features of the
resolutions embodying their conclusions will show. The
principle of federation, which forms the basis of the whole
scheme, presents the widest departure from the model
they were professedly anxious to follow. The Confederacy is not, at first at least, to assume the character
of an independent government. The executive authority,
the shape and title of which are undefined, is to be vested
in the Queen. We are thus to have a confederation of
colonies, with the Queen at their head. Whether its
chief executive officer is to be known as Governor-General,

or is to have the title and rank of Viceroy, are points apparently reserved for the determination of Parliament. All that the representatives of the several provinces undertook to determine was that the chief executive officer should be nominated by the Crown. It is of the very highest importance to the provinces that this office should be made one worthy the ambition of a statesman. The governors of Canada have necessarily, for the most part, been men of little or no mark at home. It would be very difficult to induce a rising statesman to abandon the prospects which a successful career in the House of Commons opens to him for any attractions that the Governor-Generalship of Canada, as heretofore constituted, has had to offer. At the time of the union of the two Canadas, Lord Sydenham debated in his own mind whether he should make the salary of the governor six or eight thousand pounds sterling, but the former sum was determined upon. In the near neighbourhood of the American Republic, where the chief executive officer is confined to a salary of 25,000 dollars per annum, it may easily be conceived that many of the colonists regarded the salary of their Governor-General as very extravagant; and even as late as 1849, the Legislative Assembly of Canada, in a spasmodic fit of economy, expressed the opinion that a saving in this item ought then to have been effected. As a natural consequence of this rate of remuneration, excessive as it may have seemed to a portion of the colonists, Canada has found it necessary to be content with, on the whole, an inferior order of men for governors. The two most striking exceptions have been those of Lord Sydenham and Lord Elgin. Nor is this the worst. It has happened more than once that the poverty rather than the will of the person selected for this post has induced him to accept the appointment; and the necessity for nursing the dilapidated fortunes of those functionaries has sometimes gone far to bring the representative of the Crown into discredit with the people. It is apparently to be left to our Parliament to fix the salary of the executive head of the confederation, and it is essential that, without being extravagant, it should be such as will attract men with some pretension to statesmanship.

The complexity inherent in all federations will be increased by the fact of this federation being one of colonies. Above their government, and vested with supreme sovereignty, is the authority of Parliament and the Queen; below that will be the lieutenant-governors of the provinces, deriving their appointment and receiving their pay from the federal executive. Under this tertiary authority, in Canada at least, there prevails an elaborate and an expensive, because extravagant, gradation of municipalities, beginning with the villages and ending with the aggregation of townships which form the municipality. A system of government so intricate, combining the imperial, the federative, the local, and the municipal elements, will, from its very nature, be exceedingly complex, and must be something like proportionately expensive. But there is no choice in the matter. Federation forms the only possible principle upon which British America can now be united. Lower Canada—of which a large majority of the population is of French extraction—being sensitively tenacious of its national distinctions, with the peculiar customs and rights growing out of them, could not, from its dread of absorption, be induced to assent to any closer form of union. Whether some of the other provinces might not have refused to surrender the privileges of local legislation may also be a question; for even now objections are made by the opponents of federation that the scheme exacts too great a surrender of local rights.

The relations between the Government and the chief executive officer of the confederacy will apparently differ in no respect from those which are at present subsisting between the Colonial Office and the government of any colony having representative institutions. The colonists advance with excessive timidity to whatever has the appearance of ultimate independence, and they seem to be wholly unconscious that they are framing a confederation which is to form a stepping-stone to this final end. It is not that four millions of people might not desire independence, if circumstances assured them of being able to maintain it. But the thoughtful colonist, aroused by the gigantic war which is going on in the neighbouring republic, finds it necessary to look carefully to his position on the American continent. The overshadowing predominance of a single state is the question which that war appears to him to be about to decide; for if the North can succeed in binding once more the broken fragments of the old Union, he fears an attempt to apply to the whole of Northern America the modern and exaggerated reading of the Monroe doctrine. For British America there is, therefore, no absolute independence. She must lean somewhere for support, and her inclinations, if not her interests, lead her to prefer a species of dependence upon the mother country, which shall be something more, though perhaps not much more, than a national alliance.

An ardent partisan of the perfect federative principle might find in the proposed constitution reason to object that it is not being dealt fairly by ; that under the guise of federation there lurks a manifest desire and persistent determination to establish a form of government that will in effect partake of nearly all the characteristics of a legislative union. The theory of the United States' constitution is, that the general government can exercise such powers only as are specially delegated to it by the separate states. The Quebec convention has attempted to reverse this principle by investing the confederate legislature with powers over "all matters of a general character not specially and exclusively reserved for the local governments and legislatures." Thus the residuum of unappropriated powers, whatever it may be, goes to strengthen the influence of the central government. Of the same character is the right of the federal government to appoint the local governors during pleasure. Nor will the circumstance of these functionaries being irremovable for five years, except for cause, be much, if any, check upon the centralizing tendency ; for it is not to be supposed that the federal government would want the ingenuity to have a decent pretext for the removal of an obnoxious governor. In addition to this, the general government is to have a veto on the acts of the local governments. It is impossible to mistake the direction in which these provisions point, and they are calculated to raise the question whether there exists the most perfect conformity and good faith between the semblance and essence of the yielding to local interests in the name of federation. Any attempt of this nature at overreaching would be very likely, by creating dissatisfaction, to recoil upon the masked advocates of centralization, who, in the initiatory stages, doubtless flattered themselves that they were stealing a march on the opposing principle.

The two Federative Chambers are to be respectively called the Legislative Council and the House of Commons. In the formation of the Legislative Council is another and perhaps more excusable compromise of the federal principle. It is a peculiarity of the United States' constitution that every State, great or small, is equally represented in the Senate. In this way the federative equality of all the States is maintained. The six provinces which are at first to form the British American Confederation are to be represented in the Legislative Council, not in their individual characters but in three several groups, of which the Canadas are to form one each, and the Maritime Provinces, exclusive of Newfoundland, a third. It may be perfectly just that neither Newfoundland nor Prince Edward Island should be allowed to stand on an equal footing with the great province of Upper Canada in the Legislative Council, but the disallowance of this right, nevertheless, negatives the idea of that equality which seems to belong to a perfect form of federation.

Twenty-four is the common number by which these three divisions are to be represented in the Legislative Council. A subdivision has been made for the Maritime

Provinces, under which Nova Scotia and New Brunswick are each to have ten councillors, and Prince Edward Island four. Newfoundland, which was not officially represented at the Convention, is to be allowed to enter the union with four members. The scheme embraces prospectively the entrance into the union of the North-west territory, British Columbia, and Vancouver Island, just as the articles of confederation of the thirteen colonies made provision for the admission of Canada into the United States league. These distant colonies are not parties to the scheme, and it is only stipulated that they may be admitted in the future on such conditions as the Colonial Parliament may prescribe and the Imperial Parliament sanction. Practical men could hardly talk seriously about an extension, at the present time, of the proposed union from Newfoundland to Vancouver. Between Canada and British Columbia an unsettled wilderness, across which runs the great wall of the Rocky Mountains, intervenes. Without something like continuous settlements, and, at any rate, without other facilities for travel than those which at present exist, so extended an union is out of the question. The promises of colonization made in the name of the Hudson Bay Company when it changed its proprietary, seems to have been already recalled. Add to this the disputed ownership of territory between the Company and Canada; the acknowledged want of means on the part of the proposed Confederacy to open up this country to civilization, and the hesitation of England to move in the matter, and it will be impossible to fix any probable time at which the extension of the new confederation of

British America to the Pacific will be practicable. Another obstacle may be created by such action on the part of a much-neglected colony known as the Red River Settlement as will result in its annexation to the United States. Much discontent exists among the settlers there as to their present relations with their sister colonies and the empire; and their proximity to the American border, with its pushing and hardy settlers, should obtain from them that consideration which the future, if not the present, renders advisable.

The mode of appointing the legislative councils suggested some difficulties. Of the five existing colonies three had adhered to the principle of Crown nomination; the other two, Canada and Prince Edward Island, had resorted to the principle of popular election. The delegates decided not to sanction the election by a popular vote of both Houses of the Confederate Legislature, though some among them advocated the carrying the elective principle to this extreme. It was thought that if both chambers were made elective, it would be impossible long to restrain the Legislative Council to those limits within which it has hitherto been confined; that it would demand the right to alter money bills; and that as its popular credentials would be just as strong as those of the other house, the demand could not long be resisted. Besides, it was feared that some of the overgrown electoral divisions would claim a representation more nearly in accordance with their population, and that as the principle of representation according to population was to be made the basis of the House of Commons, it might be impossible to check an encroach-

I

ment which would destroy every semblance of federal
equality in the Legislative Council. Some strange conditions have been attached to the selection by the Crown
of legislative councillors. Far from leaving the Crown
unfettered in its choice, the delegates thought it essential
to prevent the appointment of any one of immature
years to the dignified post of senator, and they decided
that no one under thirty years of age should be capable
of receiving this mark of distinction. To the qualification of age they thought fit to add one of property,
which was placed at $4,000 over all incumbrances, in
real estate. An exception, however, was made in the
case of Newfoundland and Prince Edward Island, where
the property might be either real or personal. Another
restriction on the part of the Crown, is the limiting
of the number of the councillors to eighty-two. The
reason for determining upon a fixed number was, that it
would ensure to each province a certain proportional
representation, which would be otherwise impossible.
Mr. Cardwell, in a despatch to the Governor-General of
Canada, has objected to this fixity of numbers, on the
ground that it may bring the legislative machinery to a
stand-still. There is no indication, however, that the
local legislatures, in adopting the scheme, will comply
with his suggestions to alter the provision. The Legislative Council is to be composed, in the first instance, of
persons selected from the existing local councils—a mode
of selection possibly intended to influence those bodies
in their action on the proposed scheme. Even the elected
councillors, in the provinces where the elective principle
has been adopted, will for the most part be well enough

contented with a change which relieves them from the cost and trouble of elections and the direct supervision of constituents. Strangely enough, every one of the twenty-four councillors for Lower Canada is to be held to represent a particular electoral division, in which he must either reside himself or possess the property forming his qualification. This anomalous provision was introduced for the purpose of ensuring the English minority in that province a fair proportion of representatives in this chamber. The introduction of anything like an aristocratic element into the Legislative Council will be out of the question. In framing the Constitutional Act of 1791 for Canada, Pitt proposed to establish an hereditary chamber; but though the provision continued in force till within a few years, it was never acted on in a single instance. A French traveller remarked long ago that the atmosphere of America seemed charged with democratic ideas of liberty. Their influence is not confined to the great American republic, and any attempt to improvise an aristocratic order must prove abortive.

It is one of the disadvantages under which a new country lies that has not a sufficient number of men of leisure, education, and property to fill the various legislative and executive positions. The quality of the Council is likely to be somewhat better for being selected by the Crown in the manner proposed, than it would be if elected under a suffrage so low as prevails at present. A trial of the two plans in Canada goes to show this, though perhaps not in any very striking degree. There is a contrast in the manners and habits of the two chambers in Canada. The Assembly is frequently violent and hasty; the Legislative Council is calm, dignified, but as a rule exceedingly facile, passing in an hour a measure over which the other House would wrangle for a month. The dignified indolence and quiet haste of the Legislative Council are due to the remnant of the non-elective membership, which, in spite of every new popular accession, has always sufficed to fix the character of the chamber. These qualities, perhaps, in some modified degree, will be transmitted by the proposed succession to the Legislative Council of the new confederation.

The Confederate House of Commons is to be based on the sole element of population, as determined every decade by the official census. A readjustment of the representation will take place every ten years, but no reduction is to be made in the number of members returned by any section till its population shall have decreased five per cent. relatively to the whole population of the union. The word section, as here used, is of obscure and uncertain meaning, and is capable of various interpretations. If a constituency be meant, or any number of constituencies, or a province, it would be better to say so. To Lower Canada are to be permanently assigned 65 members, and each successive readjustment is to be made up upon this standard. In the first instance, it is proposed that the House of Commons shall contain 194 members, of whom Upper Canada is to send 82, Lower Canada 65, Nova Scotia 19, New Brunswick 15, Newfoundland 8, and Prince Edward Island 5. The number may at any time hereafter be increased by the general legislature. The term for which the House is to be elected is five years—subject, of course, to be dissolved sooner if necessary. This is a longer term by one year than that for which any of the local legislatures are now elected. The extension of the parliamentary term will offer men who have neither time nor money to throw away in frequent elections in widely-spread constituencies, stronger inducements to enter public life than formerly. All laws relating to the qualification or disqualification of members, or of voters, now in force in the various provinces, are to remain undisturbed till the general legislature can supersede them by the adoption of some uniform plan.

A federative system necessarily involves something in the shape of a written constitution. It is required to define many of the powers which are respectively to be vested in the general and in the local legislatures; and to do this with such precision as to prevent any doubts afterwards arising is one of the main difficulties in the formation of such a constitution. Thirty-seven subjects of legislation are expressly named in connection with the general legislature, and eighteen only in connection with the local legislatures. The enumeration does not profess to be complete in either case, and a general clause is added comprehending all other subjects of a general or private nature, as the case may be. In some cases, including fisheries, agriculture, and immigration, a concurrent power of legislation is given. But it is evident that the power of the general government in respect of immigration will be very much restricted. The best way to attract immigrants is to offer them free grants of land.

By the terms of union the several provinces will retain the public lands; so that, with the exception of the Crown Lands of Newfoundland, which it is proposed to purchase at a figure disproportionate to their value, the general government will have no land to grant. It seems to have been regarded as impossible to make any arrangement by which the public lands of the various provinces should become vested in the general government; but surely this ought not to have been a more difficult achievement than the adjustment of so many public debts of different relative amounts. Whether any effort was made to place the public lands under the general government does not appear, but it seems to have been accepted as impossible from the outset.

The idea of numerical representation was adopted from the practice of the North American republic, as also that of decennial readjustment. The former found favour with Lord Durham when the union of the two Canadas was proposed; but the Imperial Government shrank from the possible consequences of then giving power to the French-Canadian majority. It is easy now to say that a blunder was committed; but it is very doubtful whether those who thus contend would, if the problem of 1840 had to be decided anew, have the boldness to carry that opinion into practice. The history of the agitation for numerical representation in Canada shows that it has all along been treated as a question of immediate interest rather than of principle. The Upper Canadians who strove for its adoption did not do so on the ground of its abstract merits, for they were unanimous in repudiating it so long as its operation would have told against them. This was brought to the test by a motion made by the Hon. L. J. Papineau, in 1849, for basing the representation exclusively on population. At that time Lower Canada had, or was supposed to have, the advantage in point of population, and every Upper Canadian voted against the motion. It was not till after the census of 1851 showed that the numerical balance was slightly in their favour, with a constant tendency to increase, that the demand for " representation according to population " began to be active in Upper Canada. It was advocated as a means of giving a local predominance to Upper Canada in the Legislative Assembly, to which her superior and increasing numbers seemed to give her some sort of title. But the circumstances under which the principle is now woven into the confederation scheme may, and probably will, deprive it of any such effect. The predominance of numbers under the proposed union will be against Upper Canada if she should excite the jealousy of Lower Canada and the Maritime Provinces, as they may unite together and turn against her that very weapon which she has regarded as the best means of her own defence, if not of aggression also. The system of grouping is well calculated to impress the Maritime Provinces with an idea of an identity of interest, and may possess within it the germ of future sectional strife. The deprivation of federal equality may in this way be productive of more mischief than it would had the provinces been permitted naturally to develop their federal individuality.

We have thought it necessary to comment on those features only of the scheme of union which possess general interest; there remain minor points which are merely local in their nature, but which have undoubtedly occasioned to the delegates some trouble in their elucidation. It is yet to be decided whether the scheme in its fulness shall be put into operation. There was much boldness and much danger in the resolution taken by some of the governments to carry the measure without any direct reference to the people—this kind of union, though often mooted, being, in a parliamentary sense, new. In Canada the Government felt strong enough to carry the measure without making any direct appeal to the constituencies, as the favour with which it had been received by all political parties and the absence of a strong opposition rendered it unnecessary. In New Brunswick the Government was not so sure of its ground, and a general election seemed to afford the best chance of success. Unhappily, the result of a general election has been the return of members avowedly hostile to confederation. A general election is avoided in Nova Scotia, and though the scheme of confederation is not a government measure, it is introduced into the Legislature under the paternity of their official delegates, who are thought to have sufficient authority with their own parties to ensure its adoption. Newfoundland, it is supposed, will accord her sanction to the measure, but in Prince Edward Island there is a likelihood of considerable opposition. The objections urged to the federative movement in the various colonies are for the most part of a sectional character. But there are others of more importance. It is contended that the inherent weakness of federations, as shown both in Europe and America in ancient and modern times, gives little hope of the long-continued existence of such an one as is now contemplated. But it must be considered that this federation will not be one of sovereign and independent States. The general Goverment as well as the local Legislatures will derive their authority not from a league or compact, but from the great fountain-head of power, the Imperial Parliament; and the chief executive control will be such as to counteract decentralizing tendencies. It is also feared that confederation will hasten the time when the colonies shall be separated from the mother country. Any action of this nature must proceed from the colonies themselves, as it is neither the interest nor desire of England to terminate prematurely a connexion, at least at present, to the welfare of an important portion of the empire. The growth of a lusty power on their border may perhaps lead the United States to regard it with greater jealousy than they would disunited provinces; hence it is said that there is danger to be apprehended on this score. Granting this to be the case, no one can fail to see that the individual and isolated colonies are prizes, which, if not as tempting, would at least be more easily acquired by the United States than a compact Confederacy. It is not pretended that the Confederation, with its widely-extended frontier, at many points difficult or incapable of defence, can at once stand alone. What England should do for them, and what the colonies ought to do in their own defence, are questions much debated. The ideas of the colonists are not very ambitious on the point of military expenditure, for they set out with the notion that a million of dollars a year is all they can afford. This sum will doubtless expand with their resources, or under the pressure of necessity. At present the colonists are firm in their determination to preserve their connexion with the mother country, and it is scarcely probable that the United States will drag into their Union an unwilling population on their northern boundary. They would be virtually placing their Republic between two fires. As it is, they will have trouble enough with the Southern States for a long time to come. Although there are many obstacles in the way to the formation of the proposed Confederacy, yet when, as in the present case, these are clearly perceived and calmly weighed, they cease to be hindrances which need excite apprehension. With the men of education, intellect, experience and position among the colonists nearly unanimous in support of the proposed scheme, with the Home Government cordially assenting to it, and prepared heartily to co-operate in giving it the force of law, with Parliament almost pledged beforehand to regard it with especial favour, there is no rashness in concluding that the establishment of a great British power on the American continent has ceased to be the glorious vision of a remote future, and will soon be numbered among the most splendid achievements of the present generation.

THE CANADIAN CONFEDERATION

AND THE

RECIPROCITY TREATY.*

WHATEVER differences of opinion there may be as to the advantages resulting from the connexion between England and her North American provinces, and as to which side receives the greater share, it will be generally admitted that there are disadvantages likewise attending it, and that the provinces, while participating in the former, are not at all exempt from the latter; beside being in hourly expectation of adding to their experience on the less favourable side of the account. As part of the empire, the provinces have their peculiar trials. The Fenian conspiracy, which has made itself felt in Ireland, has caused considerable uneasiness to them. Whatever the real intentions of those money-loving patriots may be, they have not hesitated to declare at public meetings throughout the United States that they purpose to conquer Canada, if not the other provinces too, and make it the base of operations against England; to seize on its shipping, and send forth from

---

* From *The Westminster Review*, October, 1866.

its ports privateers to prey on English commerce. Their numerical strength must be very great; undoubtedly they have funds at their disposal; and the object they are presumed to have in view enlists many sympathizers among all classes in the States. Officers holding commissions from the United States government are active members of the organization, and many native Americans in high official position contribute to its resources without concealment. But British Americans have troubles to contend with other than those arising from threatened Fenian attacks. The treaty of commerce which has regulated trade between the United States and the provinces for ten years past has terminated, pursuant to notice given by the former, and a new era in colonial history has been entered upon. Since this treaty, known as the Reciprocity Treaty, took effect, the trade between the two countries increased threefold; so that if it can be shown that such increase was occasioned by the treaty and is dependent upon it, it becomes a serious question to the colonists as well as to the empire, what shall be the consequence of forcing a trade amounting to $68,000,000 into new channels; and that, too, independently of the political troubles that may arise over fishery rights placed in abeyance rather than settled by the arrangement then entered into.

For some time before the existence of the treaty, the trade of the provinces was steadily growing in importance, though clogged with all the drawbacks incident to the infancy of a country having no capital, little population, and the most primitive means of communication. The sturdy backwoodsman was hewing out a home for

himself and his family, with cold and hunger held merely
at arm's length. Between him and his nearest neighbour
miles of deep forest intervened. The traveller or trader
picked his way across tangled brushwood and fallen timber, and found few finger-posts by the road side to point
out the direction in which he wished to go. The politician had his attention fully taken up with providing
for the wants of the hour; in investigating and settling
local disputes. The foundations of government were
being laid. Those political contests, which have so happily ended in the full enjoyment of constitutional liberty
and executive responsibility, were then at their height.
But as farm after farm was rescued from the woods, and
municipal institutions took shape, the consideration of
local matters widened into deliberation for the general
welfare. Schemes of internal improvement, formerly
viewed as shadowy impossibilities, grew into realities,
while bounteous harvests sent new life through every
artery of trade. Scarcely had the impulse been felt,
when English policy, impelled by Free Trade principles,
well-nigh swept away every hope that had been inspired
by glimpses of a dawning prosperity. The withdrawal
of that artificial protection which had been accorded by
the Imperial Parliament to the colonial trade forced these
provinces into the family of nations. Canada felt the
shock the most, but, imbued with a spirit of self-reliance,
at once looked about for means whereby she might
strengthen her crippled commerce. England had discrimi-
nated in favour of colonial breadstuffs and lumber, and
the provinces had imposed differential duties in the interest of the mother country. The commercial policy of

both had thus been in harmony. The repeal of the corn laws threw open to the United States a market in which the colonies had been hitherto favoured, and left the Canadians to struggle with a rival abroad which at home used every means to prevent their trade getting any headway. Canada possessed canals, but the commerce which they had been built to facilitate died on its hands, and the navigation laws then prevented foreign vessels from using them. The subsequent repeal of the navigation laws gave another advantage to the States which they have never reciprocated. The United States ship-owners were admitted to share the coasting trade of the empire, and the provinces saw, not without chagrin, American vessels both on the sea-coast and on their lakes enjoying benefits for which nothing was granted to British subjects in return. Notwithstanding the heavy duties imposed on Canadian products, a considerable trade existed between the two countries, defying every effort. to retard it altogether. Canadian wheat, being to a certain extent a necessity to the States, found its way there even under a high tariff. During the eight years prior to 1855, the year the treaty went into operation, the whole British American trade with them amounted to $138,000,000. The geographical position of the provinces, lying as they do along the northern boundary of the republic, and, wedge-like, dividing the north-western states from New England and the sea, naturally suggested the mutual advantage of closer commercial relations than had existed, and the idea of reciprocity in trade met the approval of prominent men on both sides of the territorial line. Though heavily burdened, a nucleus had formed which needed but a slight stimulus to develop itself. In the then crisis of affairs, Canada looked to this source for relief from the difficulties it found itself so suddenly plunged into, and accordingly made advances to the United States government, but a proposition for the mutual admission of certain named articles was considered by Congress as too limited. The desire was, that the other provinces should be embraced in any arrangement that might be made ; that the interest of the great north-west should be considered as regards the navigation of the St. Lawrence ; and more particularly that the Atlantic seaboard should be appeased by concessions in respect to the fisheries. Ultimately all matters in difference were satisfactorily arranged, and the Reciprocity Treaty passed into effect in March, 1855.

The expressed object of the treaty was to avoid further misunderstanding in regard to the extent of the right of fishing on the coasts of North America, and to regulate the commerce and navigation between the British American provinces and the United States in such a manner as to render the same reciprocally beneficial and satisfactory. By Article I. it is provided—

" That in addition to the liberty secured to the United States fishermen by the convention of October 20th, 1818, of taking, curing, and drying fish on certain coasts of the British North American colonies therein defined, the inhabitants of the United States shall have, in common with the subjects of Her Britannic Majesty, the liberty to take fish of every kind except shellfish on the sea-coasts and shores and in the bays, harbours, and creeks of Canada, New Brunswick, Nova Scotia, Prince Edward Island, and of the several islands adjacent thereto, without being restricted to any distance from the shore ; with permission to land upon the coasts and shores of those colonies and the islands thereof, and also upon the Magdalene Islands, for the purpose of drying their nets and curing their fish."

Article II. extended to British subjects the same rights of fishing on the eastern coasts and shores of the United States north of the 36th parallel of north latitude. This privilege has been of no benefit to the provinces, having been rarely used. In Article III. certain articles are enumerated, the growth and produce of the British colonies and of the United States, which are admitted free of duty, viz. : grain, flour, animals, meats, cotton, wool, seeds, vegetables, fruits, fish, poultry, eggs, hides, furs, skins, stone, marble, slate, butter, cheese, tallow, lard, horns, manures, ores of metals, coal, pitch, tar, turpentine, ashes, timber, lumber, firewood, plants, shrubs, trees, pelts, wool, fish-oil, rice, broom-corn, bark, gypsum, burr or grindstones, dyestuffs, flax, hemp, tow, tobacco unmanufactured, and rags. Article IV. allowed the right to United States citizens to navigate the St. Lawrence and the canals in Canada. A similar right as to the navigation of Lake Michigan was secured to British subjects. It was further agreed "that no export or other duty shall be levied on lumber or timber of any kind cut on that portion of the American territory in the State of Maine, watered by the river St. John and its tributaries, and floated down that river to the sea, when the same is shipped to the United States from the province of New Brunswick."

The extensive market unclosed by this treaty turned the tide of colonial trade to the United States, and the relieving effect was instantaneous. Since then the flow has been steady, increasing in volume year after year. The total trade under the treaty for the ten years of its continuance is estimated at $307,806,922, made up of exports to the United States of $174,865,727, and of imports $132,941,195. It may be taken for granted that the profits of this interchange were not monopolized by the provinces, as every year has brought with it an increased trade, and while they exported for the most part products of the soil, the States sent them manufactures and foreign goods mainly. The Western States suffer to a greater extent than even Western Canada, from their distance from the seaboard. The producing capacity of their vast territory is far in advance of the means of transportation. The canals and railroads of the intermediate states are totally inadequate to relieve the bursting granaries of an area which is widening year by year. The West needs additional outlets for its products, and the most natural highway by which foreign markets may be reached at the cheapest rate of transport is through the St. Lawrence. Prior to the introduction of railways, Canada saw the necessity for improving the navigation of that river for its own purposes, and, at a great expense, completed a system of canals amongst the most magnificent in the world. By the treaty, the right to use these canals was granted to American vessels, and the Western grain depots, Chicago, Milwaukee, and Detroit, were permitted to enter into direct trade with Europe. While the West had its rights thus enlarged, the special interests of the North-Eastern States were partakers also of liberal concessions. By the convention of 1818, the United States government had renounced

J

the liberty to take, dry, or cure fish, on or within three
marine leagues of any of the coasts, bays, creeks or
harbours of Canada, Nova Scotia, New Brunswick,
Prince Edward Island, and certain districts of Newfoundland and Labrador. The colonists construed this to
mean three marine leagues measured from headland to
headland, not from the coast line, and were supported in
this construction by the British Government. The
United States fishermen contended, however, for the
right to fish in any of the many bays which indent the
shores, so long as they kept three leagues from the
shore. Drawing the line from headland to headland de-
prived them of a share in the most profitable fisheries.
It was not always that this imaginary sea line was
respected by the adventurous mariners who frequented
these waters and the many detentions and confiscations
which resulted were productive of much bad feeling.
Armed cruisers, both imperial and colonial, kept a strict
look-out for delinquents, and the colonial authorities
were not tardy in the infliction of penalties for trespass
upon their rights. Had this state of things continued
much longer, it would undoubtedly have led to serious
international complications. But the treaty swept away
all disabilities, and the fishing vessels of Maine and
Massachusetts again swarmed in British waters and pursued their calling undisturbed. The value of fish taken
by them in the fisheries of the Gulf and in Canadian
waters increased from $280,800 in 1854, to $1,265,700 in
1856. Their mackerel fishery increased from 250 vessels
manned by 2750 men, and securing a catch worth $850,-
000 in the two years prior to the treaty, to 600 vessels,

employing 9,000 men and securing $4,567,500 within the two years subsequent. The Maritime Provinces were not well pleased to see their monopoly of a lucrative employment taken away, and very naturally grumbled at being forced to compete with daring and energetic intruders who had previously taken their chances outside their preserves; the more so, as the United States fishermen were backed up by bounties to the extent of four dollars per ton, while those of the provinces had no such assistance. Although the treaty was not applicable to the fisheries of Upper Canada, the vessels and fishermen of the United States were admitted to the waters and shores of Lakes Ontario, Erie, Huron, and Superior; and in 1865 took $157,504 worth of fish therefrom, while not a single Canadian vessel entered United States waters for the purpose of fishing, as the Canadian lake fisheries are by far the best. In looking back at the general results of the treaty, it will be seen, therefore, that it caused a vast expansion of a mutually profitable trade; it opened to the Eastern States a field for employment exhaustless in riches and unlimited in extent; it granted the privilege of using six canals which Canadian industry had been taxed to build; and brought into closer commercial relations two peoples, though living side by side, yet up to the time of the arrangement, knowing little of, and caring less for, each other. While it is acknowledged that the relief it brought with it was opportune and suited to the circumstances, it is not by any means admitted that the prosperity of the provinces will be seriously affected by its abrogation. At the time it went into operation, colonial trade was embarrassed but with the recovery from a temporary disturbance came a new era. The Crimean war enhanced greatly the prices of Canadian products, and thus contributed to the readjustment of business. The subsequent building of railways involved an expenditure within Canada alone of $120,000,000, so that more than one cause brought about the reaction, and more than one cause tended to its continuance. Before determining, therefore, that the commercial future of British America is at the mercy of the legislation of the United States, it would be well to compare the present with the past as regards the internal, as well as the external advancement of these colonies.

In 1851 Canada had no railways in operation; the ten years between 1850 and 1860 witnessed the construction of 2093 miles; Nova Scotia and New Brunswick have built over 300 miles also. Five years ago there were only two coal mines being worked in Nova Scotia; now there are thirty. In 1850, only 95,000 tons of coal were raised; in 1865, the yield increased to 653,854 tons. The gold product of 1865 was twenty-five per cent over that of preceding years, the amount taken out in that year being equal to $460,000; the imports have risen from $8,448,042 in 1862, to $14,381,662 in 1865; while there were exported $7,000,000 worth of her own productions—more in proportion than Canada ever sent out in one year. And this enterprising province now has 3,898 vessels of a registered worth of $13,347,500 engaged in trade. The revenue of New Brunswick in 1850 was $416,348; but in 1860 it had doubled. In one year $175,000 had been expended in building roads. The other provinces have advanced materially, every year exhibiting an increase of exports and imports. Newfoundland with its 130,000 people, of whom 30,000 are hardy sailors employed in the fisheries, has a revenue higher in proportion to the population than any of the British North American provinces.

To make the contrast plainer it will be better to take the testimony of two witnesses who cannot be charged with bias. Lord Durham in his report to the British Government on the state of the British North American provinces, said—

"By describing one side of the frontier and reversing the picture, the other would be described. On the American side all is activity and bustle. * * * But it is not in the difference between the large towns on the two sides that we shall find the best evidences of our inferiority. That painful but most undeniable truth is most manifest in the country districts through which the line of national separation passes for a distance of a thousand miles. There, on the side of both the Canadas and also of New Brunswick and Nova Scotia, a widely scattered population, poor and apparently unenterprising, though hardy and industrious, separated from each other by tracts of intervening forests, without towns or markets, almost without roads, living in mean houses, drawing little more than a rude subsistence from ill-cultivated land, and seemingly incapable of improving their condition, present the most instructive contrast to their enterprising and thrifty neighbours on the American side."

Keeping this fact in view, let us contemplate the change, as related in Mr. Derby's Report on the Reciprocity Treaty made to the Secretary of the United States Treasury, that has occurred since.

"From 1851 to 1861 the population of Canada has increased more rapidly than the population of the Union. * * * * The rate of increase in all the provinces was nearly equal to that of the Union. * * * In the fifteen years from 1851 to 1865, the whole exports and imports of Canada rose from $35,000,000 to $87,000,000. Her revenue rose also from $3,500,000 to $10,500-000. Between 1851 and 1865, her improved land increased from 7,307,950 acres to 10,855,844, or 49 per cent.: the value of the same from $263,516,000 to $466,675,780. The wheat crop, which exceeds that of Illinois and each of our States, rose from 15,756,-493 bushels to 27,274,779, or 78 per cent. The oat crop, larger than that of New York, the leading State of our Union, rose from 20,369,247 bushels to 38,772,170, or 91 per cent. During the same period the value of the lumber rose from an average of $7 to $10 per M.; and in the interval between 1851 and 1863, her exports of lumber rose from $5,085,628, of which but 23 per cent. reached the United States, to a total of $12,264,178. * * * * From 1851 to 1861 she has increased her miles of railway from twelve to nineteen hundred miles ; she has increased her wheat and oat crops, her wool, the value of her forests and wealth, *more than we have*, although she is naturally inferior in climate, soil and position."

But while the unwearying industry and praiseworthy self-reliance of the British provinces have borne fruit in a prosperity wonderful, compared even with the world's wonder, that of the United States, they have awakened " envy—the vice of republics." Those struggling and much-despised colonists have emerged from their mountains of snow and masses of ice ; from being objects of pity have attained to the lofty position of rivals. Canada has been striving fairly to make her canals and railways attract the trade of the West. In so doing she has undermined the monopoly enjoyed by the canalling and forwarding interests of Buffalo and New York, and from this source came the first complaint against the Reciprocity Treaty. The outcry was that Canada was

making " fruitless but persistent efforts to direct the
trade of the Western States from the natural channels it
had already formed." The aggrieved interests were powerful and active. The advocates of protection duties seized
the opportunity to swell the chorus that the S·ates had
the worst of the bargain, until at length the combination
of forces has succeeded in bringing to an end an agreement which has done so much for commerce, and substituted therefor a system of duties based on the exploded
fallacies of protection. No complaint was urged against
the Maritime Provinces; Canada has been the alleged
transgressor. But the charges against Canada were
coupled with objections which, according to the pro-
tectionist theories, proved the impolicy of reciprocity.
Prior to the treaty, the exports from the States to Canada
exceeded the imports thence, but in 1860 this was re-
versed, and since that time the balance of trade has been
against the States. The exports to that province fell
from $20,883,241 in 1856, to $12,842,596 in 1862, though
they again rose in 1864 to $19,589,055. This decline in
exports is attributed to several causes. It is alleged that
heavy duties were imposed by Canada upon many of the
articles the States had to sell; that discriminating tolls
and duties were laid upon their merchants and forwarders ;
that the method of levying duties on merchandize of
foreign origin has been for the avowed purpose of checking the trade of New York and Boston; and that the
whole policy of Canada is avowedly restrictive and adverse to the interests of the United States. On the other
hand the Canadians allege that the increase of these
duties was not for the purpose of discriminating against

the States, but was imposed by financial necessities, as
British manufacturers were subjected to the same burdens ;
that if they have raised their tariff, they have not reached
anything like the height of the United States tariff, which
latter has mounted fully twenty-five per cent. over that of
1854 ; that the method of levying duties on foreign merchandize is precisely similar to that of the United States as
regards goods generally ; and that the policy of Canada
has been liberal and calculated rather to attract than to
force trade.   The progress of the discussion has brought
out three classes of opponents to the treaty in the States.
Those whose interests were directly injured by it, and who
contend that Canada has violated its spirit ; those who looked upon it in the light of a political failure, separating more
widely rather than bringing together the two countries,
and who urge that its continuance is necessary to the existence of the provinces, at the same time viewing its
abrogation as a sort of chastisement for the colonial
aversion to annexation ; and those, generally, who advocate a system of high protective duties.   With faint hope
of overcoming such an union of opposing forces, but
anxious to give evidence of their desire to establish international trade on a satisfactory basis, the provinces sent
Commissioners to Washington to negotiate for the continuance of the Treaty.   In connexion with Sir Frederick
Bruce, the British Minister, the Commissioners laid the
subject of their mission before the United States Government. Mr. McCulloch, the able Secretary of the Treasury,
without any inclination to interfere with the freedom of
trade, felt called upon to consider first the requirements
of the revenue, but it was intimated that while a con-

tinuance of the treaty was out of the question, some arrangement might be made by legislation that would prove equitable. The Commissioners appeared before the Congressional Committee of Ways and Means, and after a lengthy discussion found that the demands of the Committee were so extravagant, according to provincial ideas, that it would be useless to negotiate further. While acknowledging the advantage of the treaty, the Commissioners would not admit its necessity to the provinces; and regarding the subordination of colonial legislation, in the matter of excise duties, to that of the United States, as too great a sacrifice for a very uncertain benefit, returned home to announce the failure of their mission. The firm stand taken in resistance to dictatorial arrogance, was fully approved of by the people of the provinces, and with an unanimity which must have astonished those in the United States who fancied they had got their neighbours "on the hip." From Lake Huron to the Atlantic, the result was accepted with calmness, if not with satisfaction, and the local press went earnestly to work to prepare the merchant, the farmer, and the mechanic for a new order of things. The wisdom of confederation became apparent to those who before had looked upon that scheme with coldness; and the provinces now feel they are no longer isolated settlements, but vigorous communities having interests in common which make the prosperity of one the prosperity of all. They know more of each other now, and the instincts of a common nationality urge them to provide against a common danger. Times have changed since they appeared first at Washington to solicit reciprocity in trade.

Then they were weak and poor; now they are vigorous and well to do. Then they were insignificant and spiritless; now they feel that their country has a splendid destiny, and they are ready to lay a bold hand on the commerce of more than one continent.

But let us look more closely at the principal branches of the colonial trade likely to be affected by the infliction of vexatious duties on the part of the United States. At the time the treaty was made the United States tariff on the articles mentioned in the treaty was on animals, butter, pork, fish, eggs, pelts, wheat, flour, barley, oats, rye and corn, vegetables, fruits, lumber and timber, 20 per cent.; wool, clover and coal, 30 per cent. Subsequently the rates were raised on coal, tobacco and wool. The Committee on Ways and Means, on the expiration of the treaty, proposed to increase the duties as follows: salmon, $2; mackerel, $1; herrings, 50 cents; all other pickel fish, $1 per barrel; coal, 50 cents per ton; timber, one-half cent per cubic foot, to $2 per 1,000 feet, according to variety; lumber, one-quarter cent per cubic foot to $2 per 100 feet, according to variety; animals, 20 per cent.; barley, 10 cents per bushel; beef, 1 cent per pound; corn, 10 cents per bushel; wheat, 20 cents per bushel, &c. But the House of Representatives rejected the report of the Committee on the ground that the proposed increase was not high enough to afford protection to home industry. With this object, therefore, a scale of duties was insisted upon, which satisfied the advocates of "protective policy;"—Lumber, three-quarter cent per cubic foot to $3 per 1,000 feet; stone, 35 per cent.; animals, 30 per cent.; barley, 25 cents per bushel; wool, 10 to 25 cents per pound, &c. ; but the latest advices are to the effect that no Act has yet been passed on the subject. The staples of the provinces are grain, breadstuffs, lumber, wool, coal and fish. As to the grain trade, Canada will be a loser. The treaty gave to her a home market, in which no large risks were run, and in which money was turned over very rapidly. But this branch of trade has curious features. In 1863 Canada imported from the States 5,338,095 bushels of wheat, and exported thither only 3,850,000 bushels, while its export to foreign countries was 8,969,304 bushels. A great deal of the wheat imported was exported as flour. Now, the Maritime Provinces in 1863 imported from the States 3,612,232 bushels, nearly the amount sent by Canada to the States. Nova Scotia alone, in 1865, received 2,520,819 dollars worth of flour from the States for home consumption ; so that if an intercolonial trade, hitherto neglected, can be built up, the loss of the United States market will be to a great extent repaired. Canada has the advantage, likewise, of having her flour 800 miles nearer to the lower ports than the United States, if the latter relied on the Western product. It is expected that a great deal of Canadian wheat will find its way across the lines, as its superior quality makes it acceptable to the wealthier classes. It should be considered that, owing to the ravages of the midge and the weevil, the Canadian farmer has been compelled to depend less on his wheat crop, and repeated losses have driven him to devote more attention to the breeding of cattle and the raising of the more hardy cereals, such as barley. Of barley and rye Canada sold to the States $4,500,000 worth in one year, and imported from thence $900,000 worth, while Indian corn was imported to the value of about a million. The Canadian barley is far superior to that produced in the States, and it remains to be seen whether a duty of 25 cents per bushel will keep it out, as it costs about 40 cents a bushel to transport it from the Mississippi to Buffalo, the point of competition. It is probable that the additional tax will be paid by the brewers of New York and Philadelphia. As a set-off to any loss in the grain trade, there will be the profit accruing to Canada from becoming its own carrier. Instead of sending wheat and flour to New York and to Portland, to be distributed thence to Europe and the lower provinces, it will go in Canadian bottoms by the St. Lawrence route. The lumber trade possesses within itself the guarantee of continuance. The principal export is to Great Britain. In 1865 Canada exported products of the forest to the value of $14,283,207, of which $8,996,355 went to Great Britain, and $5,008,746 to the United States. Nova Scotia in 1862 exported $611,725, and New Brunswick $2,810,-188, the latter province sending most of her lumber to foreign parts. The exhaustion of the supply of lumber in the States must render them in time dependent on the yield of the Canadian forests. It is estimated that there is, in this province alone, 287,000 square miles of pine forest and valuable wood on which to draw. The Western States, with their wide treeless prairies, cannot much longer have their wants supplied by the lumber of Michigan, nor can the Middle and Eastern States remain at the mercy of the Maine lumbermen, and must, despite of a high duty, purchase where the article is to be got. The manufacture of wool in the United States consumed 152,000,000 of pounds in 1864, nearly half of which was imported. Of the amount imported in 1865, Canada supplied $1,351,722 worth. In 1860, $15,000,000 of worsteds were imported by the States, principally from England. The Canadian wool has been found equal to the best English lustre wool, and far superior to any that can be produced in the States. So they must purchase somewhere, as the home supply is wholly inadequate to the demand, both in respect to quantity and quality. The wool going in free under the treaty has been of great assistance to their manufacturers, and its partial exclusion, if it can be excluded at all, will force the Canadians to manufacture and send woollen goods into the States. The Canadian woollen manufacturers are rapidly increasing, and New York merchants found it profitable last year to import woollens from Montreal, and that, too, after paying high duties, and suffering from exchange being against them. The Nova Scotians know that their bituminous coal can be laid down in the Atlantic cities at a price much lower than it can be brought from the United States coal districts, and a duty of $2 a ton will not exclude what can stand a $3 duty. The gas works and factories of the Eastern States require this description of coal to heat their furnaces, so that an additional tax will only render their manufacturers less able to compete with those of foreigners, without being prohibitory, and will bring into the harbours of Nova Scotia the Atlantic steamers that have been wont to coal at Boston and New York. The duties imposed on fish cannot injure the Maritime Provinces to a great extent. The exclusion of United States fishermen from a valuable fishing ground will go far to reconcile them to the loss of the treaty, as they can find a ready sale in foreign countries for all the fish they can catch. They rely upon the enterprise of their own people to extend sales in the direction of the West Indies, Mexico, and South America. Last year Nova Scotia exported to foreign countries over $3,000,000 worth of fish; and the trade of New Brunswick with the United States in this article is now nearly equalled by its trade with the West Indies. Newfoundland has its greatest source of wealth in the fisheries, but its total exports to the States amounted only to $238,645, while it imported thence $1,728,985 worth of articles, which could nearly all be advantageously supplied from Canada. To counteract the policy of the United States, the provinces have sent out commissioners to the West Indies and to Brazil, seeking to substitute new markets for that from which it seems to be determined to exclude them; and so far the prospects are encouraging.

In addition to this, they contemplate a readjustment of their tariffs so as to make their country the cheapest to live in, and the most attractive to foreign labour and foreign capital. No retaliatory measures are threatened. The disposition is to throw off every shackle that fettered trade. It is thought, therefore, and with good reason, that the disturbance of colonial trade will be but temporary. Even taking it for granted that a high protective tariff will be efficacious in sealing up the United States against the staples of the provinces, the colonists can look confidently to the establishment of an intercolonial trade, and a direct foreign trade, which shall make up for all that they have lost, and relieve them from the embarrassments of a supposed dependency.*

The political consequences of the abrogation of the Reciprocity Treaty are worthy of serious consideration. No doubt the adoption of the treaty by the United States was owing in a great degree to their expectation that a reciprocal interchange of products would cause such a mingling of interests as to lead the British provinces to regard their prosperity as inextricably bound up with the fate of the great Republic. It is now seen that the desired effect has not been produced. On the contrary, the two countries are as distinct as ever, and we are not surprised to read in what may be considered a State paper, a paragraph devoted to the question, "Can the provinces be coerced into annexation?" Mr. Derby is certainly plain-spoken. "There are," he remarks, "gentlemen of intelligence, and possibly some statesmen, who think it will be politic to allow the treaty to expire without any efforts or arrangements for renewal, who predict that in such case the provinces will range themselves under our banner, and seek admission into the Union." Canada, with its 1,000 miles of frontier, would be a valuable acquisition to them now, when they are attempting to wall themselves in by the imposition of protective duties. Canada and the lower provinces may become the distri-

---

* The Maritime Provinces will take Canadian flour, and will send in return coal and fish, without needing the United States merchants to act as middlemen. Instead of sending provincial lumber, grain and fish to New York, to be thence exported by United States shippers to Brazil, Cuba the West Indies, Hayti, Australia, Peru, and Africa, the colonist will henceforth have a greater share of the profits of the products of his own country.

buting depot for foreign goods over the whole Continent. If Canada went into the Union, the other provinces, and the vast Red River territory, could not long resist the pressure. And were Britain to lose her foot-hold in America, a non-intercourse policy, such as that advocated in the United States Senate by Senator Chandler, extending from the Rio Grande to Labrador, would carry with it serious consequences to British commerce.

It would seem that England's course in this juncture is marked out plainly enough. It is well to follow the advice of that school of political economists who would place her vast commerce—her very life blood—at the mercy of foreign nations? Who would sacrifice the advantages gained by a lavish expenditure of blood and treasure on the altar of speculative theory? Who would rely for freedom from attack on national amiability rather than on national strength? Jurists have worked out a code of international law, but their maxims, though admitted to be true and right, are not always acted on. So colonial emancipators may lay down general principles, and issue economic promises to pay, but their principles are too general to beget implicit confidence in their prophesied effects, and their promises are without guarantee. It surely is not politic for England to alienate her friends on the North American continent by leaving them to drift about at the mercy of chance. It is admitted on both sides of the Atlantic that the existing relations between the mother country and those American dependencies must sooner or later undergo some change. When that change shall take place, or what shall be its nature, are questions yet to be decided. The decision may rest with the parties immediately interested; perhaps it may be taken out of their hands. The tie so provocative of wrath on the part of Colonial emancipators has lost the character of a Gordian knot. Its intricacy and firmness are no longer a challenge to ingenuity. No oracle need be consulted as to the secret of its undoing, as all that is required is to destroy the mutual affection which keeps the line "taut," and there will be plenty of willing hands to cast off the shore ends. The writer does not propose to deal with those who advocate an immediate and total separation as being for the best interests of both parties, and have sufficient faith in their own logic to render them easy as to the consequences. However disinclined to admit the soundness of their arguments, we must accord them that respect which earnestness based on honesty of purpose demands. But, on the other hand, there are those who go half-way with both sides in this discussion, not professedly or for any great length of time, but openly enough and sufficiently long to earn the cordial dislike of all really in earnest. This Ishmaelitish class has its representatives in the press and in Parliament. Their ability is indisputable; their influence not to be despised. Their seeming impartiality in the distribution of favours, and their sprightly readiness to break a lance with all comers, renders their specious logic and plausible statements all the more insidious and fraught with all the greater danger to those who adopt opinions second-hand on subjects not sufficiently interesting to induce personal investigation. What British Americans want is simply fair play. They have no desire to appear every other day at the bar of public opinion to answer charges that are

K

without foundation, and at the same time do not wish that judgment should be taken against them by default. The majority of them view the existing connexion as mutually beneficial and worthy of preservation. They have a dislike to absorption in the American Republic; and the circumstances in which they are placed, as well as the recollection of what they have endured to preserve their allegiance, naturally prompt them to look across the ocean for some recognition of their steadiness of purpose. They find very little satisfaction in the dictatorial utterances, and still less in the scoldings that come from this side of the water. It is not unfair for them to ask that those who assume to lead public opinion in the mother country should avoid misstating facts, whether intentionally or through ignorance, and guard against becoming uncharitable when they should be quiet. Lack of correct information can no longer be pleaded as an excuse for departure from truth, as the means of supplying it are available. Such books as that of Mr. Russell, the *Times'* correspondent, on " Canada, its Defences, Condition, and Resources," are well calculated to dispel those illusions which have led so many Englishmen to lavish their compliments on the United States and their satire on the British American provinces. Comparisons have been made to the prejudice of these colonies, and forcible lectures are still read to them on their want of energy, their mercenary spirit, their hysterical lip-loyalty, and their inclination to sponge on the imperial exchequer; the weak places in their armour are gloated over and pointed out to the world; and ready writers exercise themselves wonderfully to prove that the provinces are

wholly incapable of defence. It is not difficult to ridicule hearty expressions of attachment, nor does it require great cleverness to fling off the words lip-loyalty.
Those who so glibly utter the reproach forget what it
is they are striking at. The citizen of the United States
has a flag cf his own, and a nationality of his own,
but the provincialist has ever had to look abroad for
his. British policy isolated the colonies to prevent their
absorption in the Republic, and in so doing stunted the
growth of a native national sentiment. The American
revolution drove into the Royal provinces those who had
wished to preserve their allegiance to Britain, and the
exiles carried with them the recollection of injuries sustained and losses endured for a cause which they, foolishly or wisely, deemed worthy of the sacrifice. They gave
up houses, lands, kindred, and the associations of youth,
and exchanged comfort and ease for the dangers and
hardships of an inhospitable wilderness. The chivalrous
sense of honour which rendered them exiles was imparted
to their children. Loyalty to Britain became to them a
synonym for connexion with the mother-land and non-
adherence to the Republic. When Englishmen, therefore,
undertake to cast reflection on a loyalty that has so frequently proved itself a reality, they should first consider
what the British American means when he makes boast
of his "loyalty." Now that British America has become
prosperous and united, and the traditions of the past are
gradually losing their hold on the imaginations of a new
generation, that sentiment which so long found an outlet
in declamation over the glories of the mother-land, will
draw a more natural nourishment from native sources.

It remains to be seen what shall take its place, and whether the doling out of so much gratitude for so much benefit received will be more acceptable to English critics than the hereditary romantic attachment which allowed no danger, no loss, no neglect to sully its purity. Notwithstanding the assertion that Canada is incapable of defence, the very same persons who give it currency are among the first to charge the colonists with an unwillingness to sink in fortifications the money they need to open up roads and deepen their canals. Although the provinces have more men in training in proportion to their population than England, and that too in a country where the duty of a volunteer partakes little of the nature of play, they are sneered at for not preparing to defend themselves. What is the fact? Military schools have been established in the provinces under the superintendence of officers of the regular army, and last fall Colonel McDougall inspected in camp, at Montreal, 2,000 graduates who formed, according to his acknowledgment, as fine battalions, both in respect to physique and drill, as he, with all his experience, had ever seen. Throughout all the provinces the volunteers are regularly drilled by sergeants of the regular army in the pay of the colonists. But it may be asked, Can the fighting material be furnished? It is not necessary to call the roll of British Americans who have done battle for Britain in all parts of the world, to point to Williams of Kars, or Inglis of Lucknow, or young Dunn, who bore off the Victoria Cross from the bravest of the immortal "six hundred," or young Reade, who, though a surgeon, won the same token of heroism at Delhi, or the many others who have died under the Red Cross, Look back to the time when Maine called out her militia to settle the boundary question by force, and New Brunswick and Nova Scotia sprang to arms with but a regiment or two of British troops to assist them in rolling back the tide of invasion. In 1812, did any of the provinces quail? or did those 1,000 raw French-Canadian militia under De Salaberry, when they defeated 7,000 United States infantry at Chateauguay, show themselves deficient in bravery? At the time of the Trent affair, was there a display of timidity? At two o'clock in the morning of the eighth of March, 1866, a call was made by telegraph from the Canadian capital for 10,000 men to line the frontier, as an attack by American Fenians was apprehended; by night that number of thoroughly-equipped and well-drilled volunteers were at their respective headquarters. Stores and factories were emptied and farm houses deserted, and Canada, from Sarnia to Quebec, wore the appearance of a vast military encampment. Were double the number required, they could have been had on the same notice. And this is the Canada that has been so often scolded for not showing, according to the notions of British writers and British speakers, a willingness to defend itself!

It has been said that the provinces are mercenary and disposed to shirk taxation, but it is evident that the imposition of high taxes would be a deadly blow to their future prospects. They wish not only to retain their own population, but to be able to offer inducements to emigrants; and now that the United States have been compelled to submit to an oppressive load, there is hope that the tide of emigration will turn in favour of the provinces. Their best defence, after all, is population. With an increase in the number of inhabitants will arise an increase of wants, and capital will follow in the train. The Republicans are determined, if they cannot totally exclude British manufactures, to make British capital invested in the States pay a share of their war debt. Massachusetts has imposed a tax of four per cent. upon the receipts for premiums of all foreign insurance companies doing business in that State. The State of New York passed an Act whereby her foreign bondholders would be compelled to take their interest in United States currency when one dollar in gold was worth two dollars and a half in currency. The Supreme Court of this State has lately decided, under the Legal Tender Act, that a promise to pay in gold or silver dollars is fulfilled by a payment in "greenbacks" without the discount. British capital has been lavished on the United States. It has built their railways and canals, and sustained their different State Governments; while, strange to say, American capital has sought investment in the British provinces. The collieries of Nova Scotia, the gold mines of Nova Scotia and Canada, the copper mines of Canada, Upper and Lower, and the Upper Canadian oil wells are all for the most part in operation through capital invested in them by citizens of the United States. It is the best policy, therefore, for Canada to keep down taxation, and Canadian statesmen are wise in their generation in paying little heed to those who would urge them into spending their strength for nought.

But the cavils and scoffs, though based on fallacies, of those who have taken on themselves to lecture the provinces for alleged shortcomings, are productive of injurious consequences. A young country is particularly sensitive to outside criticism, and the fact of being a dependent, although but in name, does not blunt the edge of harshly-worded rebuke. Even the United States smarted under the attacks of a foreign press, so that the British American may be excused if he displays somewhat of a similar weakness. It is easy to laugh at him when with pardonable vanity he examines English opinion for some word of encouragement, some tribute to his industry and his endurance. The boy who leaves the home of his childhood in search of fortune looks forward with eagerness to the day when he can return laden with the fruits of his labour; and, when he has secured the reward of industry, exhibits it nowhere with so much pride as at the old homestead. The emigrant in the backwoods feels a strange pleasure in writing " home," as he continues through life to call the land of his birth, the history of his struggles and his success. It may be a mere sentiment, utterly ridiculous in the eyes of the philosophic economist, but it is human nature. It is not difficult, therefore, to imagine the feelings of the British American as he thinks of his precarious position in the American continent; of the power of the Republic that well nigh overshadows his country with its greatness; of the strong inducements held out to ambition across the lines; of the mingling of interests that makes him a participator in the misfortunes of his republican neighbours, if not an equal sharer in their prosperity; and then reads in the columns of acknowledged organs of public opinion what they say in England of himself and his home. Far away from the motherland, three thousand miles across the sea and a thousand miles inland, the Canadian tries to sift from the metropolitan press the real sentiments of the English people; and, within sight of the Stars and Stripes, peruses British journals and British reviews (not those of the United States) in which threats, ridicule, unfair comparisons, and even contemptuous disdain mark the passages that bear on his case. He may well ask, What is the object of such a mode of attack? Were British America convinced that Britain desired an immediate separation, objection from abroad would be silenced, however impolitic the step might be considered. But British America wants time. It is not ready to stand alone, as that system of colonial rule which divided the provinces and discouraged intercommunication, has produced effects which cannot be got over at once. Besides, the locking in of Canada from the sea by Lord Ashburton, which, according to Mr. Russell, "weakened Canada at its weakest point, and conferred most signal advantages on the only enemy it had to fear," and further, "bit into the substance of the provinces, and at the same time cut the vein of communication with the sea for five long winter months," must, for some time at least, prove a tremendous disadvantage. But it is quite possible that a premature dissolution of the connexion may be forced on, and it is within the bounds of probability that the separation may be associated with bitter feelings; that wounded pride and rejected affection may smother the recollections of former benefits and sympathy. No British American wishes that it should be so; surely no patriotic Englishman desires it.

DOWN THE ST. LAWRENCE ON
A RAFT.*

A HOLIDAY cruise on a timber raft does not, at the mere mention of it, suggest first thoughts of a very favourable character. It would not probably move the "old salt" to enthusiasm, or rouse the spirit of *dilletanti* yachtsmen. But a little reflection by a staid landsman not given to nautical exploit save in the mildest forms; not gifted with a levelness of head sufficient to warrant the climbing of masts, or physical control adequate to the exigencies of a rolling sea; will convince him, at least, that there are some peculiar features, some characteristic attractions connected with such a mode of seeking diversion, which recommend it as worthy of consideration. Travel by raft has no tourists, no guidebooks, no flaming advertisements to laud, or even to indicate the advantages it possesses over the usual modes of transit; so it must of necessity look for patronage to those who are fond of meditation, are not in a hurry, and are content with occasional spells of excitement. The ordinary summer tourist, who does the St. Lawrence and other fashionable routes in a steamboat, and fancies that

---

* From the *Canadian Monthly*, October, 1874.

the chief end of man has been attained, the cup of
pleasure has been drained to the dregs, and enjoyment
penetrated to the kernel, will welcome with gratitude
the information that there is a world of novelty yet unconquered, and a means of slacking a thirst for sensation
yet untapped.   But this ordinary tourist must not give
way to extravagant ecstasy at the announcement; the
charms of raft travel are for the few, not the many ; and,
as has been hinted, the capacity to discover and appreciate them is limited by conditions of an onerous character.   However, there are palpable advantages in favour
of the raft tourist over those enjoyed homeopathically by
the steamboat passenger. Fashion does not sit enthroned
on a raft ; its behests are there ignored, and the needs
of the occasion alone control.   Hence little luggage
is required, and the freedom from encumbrance which
this secures signifies lightness of heart, the natural
consequence of exemption from the importunities of
zealous hotel-porters, and energetic hackmen, as well as
a total immunity from the agony which accompanies the
crashing and smashing of one's best and perhaps only
trunk.   The raftsman on his voyage does not have his
temper tried by the impertinence of waiters, which, apart
from its moral worth, is a boom only appreciable to its
full extent by the steamboat passenger desirous of culti-
vating a relish for his victuals. He is not compelled to
appease his appetite at the expense of his manners by
being compelled to fight his way to his meals under
penalty of languishing in semi-starvation until the third
table is rung up. He is not driven to decide between
dyspepsia-producing beefsteak and a variety of dry

delicacies which give the table of a steamboat a unique, a too familiar, a never-to-be-forgotten appearance; or to strain the axis of his mind in the endeavour to decide fairly between the merits of the tea and the coffee, or to arrive at a definite conclusion respecting their similarities and differences. He is not moved to bitter envy by witnessing nice distinctions drawn between those who shall get state-rooms and those whose fate it is to be accommodated with spaces under the piano or on the dining table; nor is his bachelorhood, if so it be, put to open shame by a curt negation of its claims to attention until everybody else is told off. He is not kept awake at night by the giggling of girls, nor put to sleep in the day-time by their incessant chatter. No! the raftsman is his own waiter. He takes his meals when prompted to eat by a natural hunger which does not come and go at the sound of the dinner-bell; his place at table is anywhere and everywhere he chooses to sit; his diet is simple,—pork, hard-tack, bread, potatoes, tea undisguised by chalk-milk and untoned by sanded sugar, and game, sometimes, such as the hen-houses along the shore deliver into his piratical grip; his sleeping apartment is a shanty of pine boards specially built for airiness, and capable of coming down at a moment's notice; his bed, consisting of two military blankets and a valise pillow, is always ready made; his tub is the river, ever at hand; his "constitutional" is on wood pavement, ever free from dust. He has abundant leisure to view the scenery; he can read, write, talk and walk, or sleep, just as he pleases, and in fine, is as nearly his own master as he can well be. The sense of complete freedom expands his chest, and no un-

trammelled son of the desert can experience more complete buoyancy of spirit than does the shaggy unkept
tourist who drinks in the fresh morning air as he
saunters up and down a 100-foot log in the middle of the
river, or, extended at full length, basks in the sunshine
listening to the plash of the waves as they gently lave
the sides of his raft. So that a comparison between the
two modes of travel shows advantages on the side of the
seemingly less enjoyable, which in their æsthetic, dietetic,
social and moral character, go to mellow the hard feeling
incident to first thought on the subject of raft navigation.   Were it desirable to depress the scale too much in
favour of the raftsman's view, it would be open to his
sympathizers to throw in the continuous opportunity for
fishing which the steady movement of the raft furnishes,
—but some unoccupied ground must be left to the
imagination.

The raft is quite safe so long as its constitutent logs
keep together.   Should it resolve itself, or be resolved
into its elements in deep water, danger is to be apprehended, for every one cannot walk on, or even keep
astride of, a log in the water.   Blondin and Blondinists
could perhaps ; but unaccustomed raftsmen find it rather
slippery work.   Any one who is perfect at paddling a
tub could hold his own on a log ; but the tendency to
roll is a source of such danger to the isolated squatter
on square timber, as to justify a casual observer in mis-
trusting its efficiency as a life-preserver.   Walking on a
detached log means not a succession of steady steps, but
a movement akin to what one understands by St. Vitus'
dance.   The raft proper is composed of what are techni-

cally called drams, each of which is a complete raft in
itself; in fact a raft is a number of drams chained or
roped together.   The timber intended to be rafted down
to Quebec is taken from the booms, say in Toronto bay,
and built up in drams.   Huge sticks of pine, ash, elm, or
oak, are laid side by side to the width of about fifty-two
feet, and to the length of about two hundred and fifty
feet, with a space of two feet between the ends of the
logs, so as to give them room to play in a rough sea;
these are bound to traverses, or cross-pieces, laid every
three feet, by withes of young ironwood, oak or hickory
trees rendered pliable by a twisting machine.   The bottom being thus laid, it is loaded in tiers until the dram
draws from three-and-a-half to six feet of water, according to the quantity or weight of timber.   A shanty is
built of pine boards on the middle of the dram, and the
dram thus honoured is called the Cabin Dram; the cook's
house adjoins the shanty, and in it are stored barrels of
pork, biscuit and bread.   Around the bow, stern and
sides of the dram, rullocks are constructed at an eleva
tion of three feet, and oars thirty-six feet long and about
fifty pounds weight are provided.   It takes fifteen men
a month to build one of these drams. For going through
the canals, the drams are built about twenty-four by one-
hundred and twenty, and in a less secure manner than
those intended to take the chances of the rapids.   It is
said to be as cheap to take a raft through the canals as
down the river, and the more valuable timber, such as
oak and pine, goes by the former route, as the risk of
loss is of course much diminished.   One wonders why
all the timber does not go through the canals, when the

dangers of the rapids are taken into consideration, and it is remembered that no insurance companies extend their ægis over the timber man. If a dram sticks on a shoal, or is run on the beach, it takes a deal of pulling and hauling to get it off again, the cost oftentimes being from two to five hundred dollars. When everything is ready, the drams are lashed together, two and two, and a tugboat steams off with them down Lake Ontario, and thence along the river St. Lawrence to Prescott.

The distance between Toronto and Kingston was accomplished in eighty-five hours, and the captain of the *Edsall* felicitated himself on the speed and strength of his tug, but expressed regret when he recollected that his vessel was paid according to the time occupied, that is, about $200 a day. Eighty-five hours between Toronto and Kingston (one-hundred-and-sixty-five miles), is a good long time to an "amateur casual," on a raft though to a timber man it represents a short raft passage between the points named. Three days of sunshine, three days of gossip with the men, three days devoid of stirring incident, save a slight blow which set the timber creaking in a manner sufficiently startling to give a good idea of what a storm could do if it only chose. To a timber raft badly put together, a storm on the lake means "scatteration" in its most destructive sense, and a log hunt for a month afterwards. But our parallelogram went quietly and smoothly onward. The men slept and ate, and ate and slept during the day, and sat up all-night telling stories, singing songs and dancing. All nationalities were represented, but the French and English-speaking Canadians especially vied with each other

in tales of adventure and the recital of personal
experience. There was Antoine, who had laid the axe to
the roots of great trees in Western Canada and in Michigan, and was now on his way to his domicile of nativity.
His had been a life of hard labour, speckled with oases
of romance, and seemed nothing loath to pass it in
panoramic review for the entertainment of his fellows ;
but his forte was, like a true sentimentalist, music. He
sang, with an air of resolution, the songs of French
Canada, and when incited to melody showed a wonderful skill in giving his voice the *tremolo* much affected by
popular singers, thus realizing Charles Lamb's description of the piping of the gentle giantess. "The shake
which most singers reserve for the close or cadence, by
some unaccountable flexibility or tremulousness of pipe
she carrieth quite thro' the composition, so that her time
to a common air keeps double motion—like the earth
running the primary circuit of the tune, and still revolving on its own axis." His favourite air, and indeed that
of all, was the canoe refrain, *En roulant ma 'boule*, the
chorus of which was rendered with great spirit, its
accompaniment being a violent working of the arms, intended to represent paddling. The words of this song
extend over thirteen verses, so a few will suffice as
specimens :—

> Derrièr' chez nous, ya-t-un étang,
>   En roulant ma boule (*chorus*),
> Trois beaux canards s'en vont baignant
> Rouli, roulant, ma boule roulant,
> En roulant ma boule roulant (*chorus*)
>   En roulant ma boule.

Trois beaux canards s'en vont baignant
En roulant ma boule,
Le fils du roi s'en va chassant,
Rouli, roulant, ma boule roulant,
En roulant, etc.

Le fils du roi s'en va chassant
En roulant ma boule,
Avec son grand fusil d'argent,
Rouli, roulant, ma boule roulant,
En roulant, etc.

Then there was Pierre, who was making his yearly pilgrimage to his home, or rather his wife's home—for poor Pierre had been blessed with a shrew, and like the simple-minded fellow he is, took to the woods every fall, worked hard all winter chopping, and about midsummer found himself again rafting towards the consumer of his wages. His matrimonial felicity was not perfect, as a week under the roof of his little white-washed cottage seemed to render him equal to another year's absence, another year's endurance of cold and shanty hardship, another year's experience on pork diet. Hugh, the cook, had his budget of songs of the "Mother Darling" class, as well as of the dramatic, which were made to tell by the addition of fanciful bits of clog dances, while his border tales were of the most incredible kind, fearful robberies of fowl, and dreadful legends as to the eating capacity of the winter shanty men. The foreman of the raft was a mine of statistics, and full of interesting details as to the lumber trade, which he prefaced with a characteristic song, descriptive of the raftsman's life—

Voici l'hiver arrivé ;
Les rivières sont gelées ;
C'est le temps d'aller au bois
Manger du lard et des pois.
Dans les chantiers nous hivernerons !
Dans les chantiers nous hivernerons !

Pauv' voyageur que t'as d'la misère !
Souvent tu couches par terre,
A la pluie, au mauvais temps
A la rigeur de tous les temps.

Quand tu arrive à Québec,
Souvent tu fais un gros bec
Tu vas trouver ton bourgeois.
Qu'est là, assis au comptoi'.

——Je voudrais être payé
Pour le temps que j'ai donné.
Quand l'bourgeois est en banq'route,
Il t' renvoi manger des croûtes.

Quand tu retourn' chez ton pere,
Aussi pour revoir ta mère ;
Le bonhomme est à la porte,
La bonne femme fait la gargotte.

——Ah ! bonjour donc, mon cher enfant !
Nous apport'-tu ben d'l' argent ?
——Que l' diable emport' les chantiers !
Jamais d' ma vie j'y r'tournerai !

In his less musical moments the foreman becomes communicative, and is nothing loath to tell respecting his operations in the woods, his hauling the logs to water, his draining lakes to gorge the shallow streams and rivers down which they float the logs, and to give,

L

with dates and items, all the minor details which go to make up his business life. His information is varied, and he appreciates at its true value the great forest. From him we learn such facts as the following: Canada possesses almost every variety of ornamental wood, and at great International Exhibitions displays not less than sixty-four varieties of timber. The great variety of kinds, and the abundance in quantity of our forest woods, is the reason that the greater number of them have no intrinsic value here. Oak, pine, walnut, maple, elm, tamarack, and cedar, are our chief exports. Last year the total exported produce of our forests reached $28,586,816 in value, the largest quantity being of white pine. Next in value come Agricultural Products, and after them Animals and their produce. At the late lumberers' convention at Ottawa, Mr. Little stated that the forests of the United States and Canada, taken together, will not afford a supply of white pine for more than twelve or fifteen years at the utmost, at the present rate of consumption. Such a statement carries with it a significance which those who look into the future would do well to ponder over. The exhaustion of Canadian forests means the loss of our chief source of export. But the rapid consumption going on signifies to the lumber-man that every year his work will be further and further back from civilization, and that his hardships, if not his wages, will steadily increase.

The hours went very slowly in doing Lake Ontario's, 180 miles, but the leisure thus afforded to familiarize oneself with the men, and to admire the sticks of timber, the excellencies of which were repeatedly pointed out was, as may be seen, somewhat improved. Once through the lake and past Kingston, it might be supposed that the scenery of the Thousand Islands would dispel the langour which had at times manifested itself in all. Though willing to answer when questioned, the rafts-man, like the Indian, is never garrulous. Gazing at the waves as they ripple by with sunshine pillowed on their tiny crests, or lazily watching the shore where the doz-ing hills nodded a seeming recognition with their cloud night-caps, he yielded him to the soporific spirit of the scene, and became silent, dreamy, and sometimes even sleepy. Nepenthe has been found. Even the Thousand Islands, with their luxuriantly tinted foliage, their over-hanging branches, and dainty bowers, their myriad forms of substance and shadow, their winding passages, their delightful change of landscape, their seventy miles of lingering sweetness—all, all failed to dispel torpor or awaken into activity the ratiocinative faculties. We gazed and enjoyed and gazed and dozed. The solitude, the stillness, the exquisite beauty of the scene, the balminess of the atmosphere, intoxicated like sweet incense, and stole away all sense of life ; dreamland with its figments and pigments was ours, and for many a mo-ment, a set of beings happy and contented as ever roam-ed the Elysian fields, were the somnambulists of our raft. Our sleep was not dull, heavy, abject uncon-sciousness, but rather delicate, soft, quiescence—rest to the body, holiday to the mind. The griefs and dis-appointments of the past clothed themselves in wedding garments and danced like dervishes *vis-à-vis* to the joy-ous possibilities of the future. In truth, the Thousand

Islands were to us the Thousand-and-one Nights of oriental fiction. But this somniferous delirium was too painfully delicious to last, and, like everything mundane, came to an end. At Prescott we were restored to the consciousness of life's realities by the departure of the steam tug, and beneath the shadow of the famous old wind-mill which had witnessed some of the pranks of '37, the drams shook off the coils that had so long united them, and each made ready to do for itself in its down-ward course. Pilots came on board, huge oars were shipped, men were hired in quantities, fifteen or sixteen to a dram, and after a few strokes from the long oars, which looked amazingly like monstrous *antennæ*, our raft was in the current moving along with a speed startling in its contrast to the former creeping motion. The rapids now began to be referred to with respect, and even the current, as it swept our parallelogram around islands, through narrow channels, shaving shoals and rocks that looked uninvitingly near, became a subject of conciliatory compliment. Steady work at the oars had taken the place of indolence, and the men shout to each other in French, Indian and English; brisk repartee and stentorian laughter indicate rising spirits; and the timid tourist, partaking of the general excitement, leaps from log to log for the purpose of reassuring himself as to their adhesive qualities, and recalls the lines of Sangster :

> " All peacefully gliding,
> The waters dividing,
> The indolent bateau moved slowly along.
> The rowers light-hearted,
> From sorrow long parted,
> Beguiled the dull moments with laughter and song.

' Hurrah for the rapid ! that merrily, merrily
  Gambols and leaps in its tortuous way ;
  Soon we will enter it, cheerily, cheerily,
  Pleased with its freshness and wet with its spray.'

    " More swiftly careering,
      The wild rapid nearing,
They dash down the stream like a terrified steed ;
     The surges delight them,
     No terrors afright them,
Their voices keep pace with the quickening speed :
 ' Hurrah for the rapid ! that merrily, merrily
  Shivers its arrows against us in play ;
  Now we have entered it, cheerily, cheerily,
  Our spirits as light as its feathery spray.'

    " Fast downward they're dashing,
      Each fearless eye flashing,
Though danger awaits them on every side ;
     Yon rock—see it foaming—
     They strike—they are drowning !
But downward they speed with the merciless tide :
  No voice cheers the rapid, that angrily, angrily
  Shivers their bark in its maddening play,
  Gaily they battled it—heedlessly, recklessly,
  Mingling their lives with its treacherous spray ! "

The river has a glazed appearance ; its very oiliness indicates something wrong under the surface; the revolving
eddies in their corkscrew movements predicate trouble
ahead ; and the accelerated speed of the raft forewarns
one of danger that lurks not far in the distance. We are
beginning to go down hill very swiftly. No wonder.
From Lake Erie to Montreal, 367 miles, the descent is
564 feet. Vessels coming up through the seven canals
constructed to avoid these St. Lawrence rapids ascend

116 miles of river in actual horizontal distance, overcoming a fall of 225 feet above the level of the tide water, and this in a river said to discharge 4,300,000 tons of fresh water annually into the ocean. So there is good reason for our raft making good time onwards—it is going down the first pair of stairs. But the white caps of the Galops have little temper for us as we plough through, for the tumble of this rapid is less fierce than we, in our innocent excitement, anticipated. Not a stick is displaced, and confidence in the buoyancy and strength of our platform rises several degrees. Grown bolder by slight experience, we express loudly our desire to encounter the famous Long Sault, the most magnificent of all the rapids, and whose dangers were, in the olden time, especially dreaded. Says Mr. Boulton, in his topographical description of Upper Canada (1824): "Boats may pass near shore, but where misfortune has driven either a boat or a raft into the very strong part of the current, it hath seldom happened that a life has been saved. A melancholy instance of the danger of this occurred in the late French war, when several boats and their crews were entirely lost." But enquiries of an historical nature were cut short abruptly, after reaching smooth water again, by the appearance of a canoe which angled towards the raft for a while, and finally succeeded in coming alongside. Its passengers were two Indians, a white-haired old gentleman, evidently papa, and a fair-faced girl, evidently papa's daughter. The transfer of this new and unexpected freight to the cabin-dram was a work of short duration, and thence an explanation of the angelic visit was soon promulgated, to the effect that daughter

had long cherished an "intense, eager, and insatiable
longing" to "shoot the rapids," and that papa had in-
sured his life, and given reluctant consent on one condition, viz. : that he should accompany her. She carried a
dainty satchel containing wine-biscuits for nibbling purposes, and papa, like a sensible man, displayed anxiety
respecting the movements of substantial hampers, which
the keen-scented cook followed about with radiant coun-
tenance. The new arrivals occasioned much excitement.
The Indians at the oars betrayed no sign, save that their
black eyes flashed for an instant. The French grimaced
at each other. The English slapped their knees violently
but said nothing. The surprise was too much for vocal
expression. Never had such a thing been dreamed of in
raftmen's annals as the shooting of the Long Sault by a
young lady. She was not very strong looking, but she
had delicate features, long wavy hair which fluttered
gaily in the breeze, a *petite* figure, and eyes full of
sunshine and sweetness. It seemed to grow on us that
she was neither merry nor giddy; her demeanour rather
bespoke characteristics such as thoughtfulness and kindness. When she seated herself on a coil of hawser, and
quietly took to her "tatting," to the discomfiture of some
on board who would have been glad to furnish her with
full statistics relative to the dimensions of the canals, and
to point out to her the peculiar excellencies of the various
sticks of timber, the oarsmen looked very knowing and
sarcastic. Some persons transferred their valuable information and services to papa, who showed his appreciation
of several hours' run of learned conversation by breaking
out in the middle of a table of condensed mathematics,

with an allusion to his hampers. The allusion was caught up with alacrity, and a motion toward the victuals had a seconder in everybody not engaged at the oars. The contrast between hard-tack and sponge-cake is great! The gulf between fat pork and chicken is vast! A land appetite and a water appetite are totally different things! *Aqua vitæ* and *aqua fortis* have nothing in common. The little lady was somewhat sly, for no sooner were potations ended than she demanded a song. Each looked at the other; one had a cold; another had left his music at home; but silence was cut short by the irrepressible Antoine, who looked tenderly at the maiden, then ferociously at his companions, and sang out to a delicious minor air:

Isabeau se promène
Du long de son jardin,
Du long de son jardin.
   Sur le bord de l'ile,
  Du long de son jardin ;
    Sur le bord de l'eau,
    Sur le bord du vaisseau.

Elle fit une rencontre
De trente matelots,
De trente matelots.
   Sur le bord de l'ile, etc.

Le plus jeune des trente
Il se mit à chanter, etc.

—La chanson que tu chantes
Je voudrais la savoir, etc.

—Embarque dans ma barque,
Je te la chanterai, etc.

Quand elle fut dans la barque,
Elle se mit à pleurer, etc.

—Qu'avez-vous donc la belle,
Qu'avez-vous à pleurer ? etc.

Je pleure mon anneau d'or
Dans l'eau il est tombé, etc.

Ne pleurez point la belle,
Je vous le plongerai, etc.

De la troisième plonge,
Le galant s'est noyé,
Le galant s'est noyé.
　　Sur le borde de l'île,
　Le galant s'est noyé
　　　Sur le bord de l'eau,
　　　Sur le bord du vaisseau.

This melancholy story was quickly ousted from memory by other and more lively airs, so that the impromptu pic-nic was a great success. The little lady looked pleased, and laughed right merrily when her experiments on hard-tack resulted in a vain endeavour to indent it with her pearly molars and incisors. An offer to file her teeth to the requisite sharpness was declined with a profusion of thanks which abashed the offerer as completely as if he had been smothered in rosebuds. Further enjoyment of the festive occasion is cut short by the announcement that the rapids are near. The pilots take their position, and in a few moments the drams, one after another, spring forward with fearful velocity, and plunge violently into the breakers of the Long Sault. The waves leap to the encounter as if they would dash themselves over the restless timber, but exhausted by their own fierceness, tumble headlong in masses of white foam. The dram stops, a convulsive throb gives motion seemingly to every fibre of

the timber—but it is for an instant.   The pilot shouts;
the men strike their oars deep in the water, and the dram,
like an expert surf-diver that it is, takes a header through
the loftiest breaker ; the bow oarsmen drop on their
knees and cling to the traverses.   For a few seconds they
are lost to sight in tempests of spray, while an undulat-
ing spasm seizes the dram and runs through its entire
length, causing every portion in turn to heave and toss
like a wounded serpent, and straining every withe to its
utmost tension.   But the stoppage is momentary.   Again
the all-powerful current clutches the dram, and, rendered
more fierce by impediment, drags us onward, down narrow passages between rocks, over precipices of water, past
threatening shoals, cutting the crest from pyramids of
surge, and riding victor-like upon clouds of sparkling
spray until, wearied with triumph, we lose all consciousness of the hydra-headed dangers lurking on every side,
and give fancy and imagination free rein to revel in the
sights of grandeur and beauty which flit before our eyes
like an enchanted panorama.

It is hard to say who of the non-raftsmen exhibited the
most equal courage during the passage, but, though she
had sat by herself in the middle of the dram, had looked
very pale, trembling very much, and let slip a few tears
when the last white cap was left astern, the little lady
was pronounced by unanimous vote to be a true raftsman ; and several sun-burnt, big-shouldered fellows carried a large stick of timber near to where she sat (which
they shortly brought back again), to secure the opportunity of whispering to her, " You are a trump, miss."   At
any rate when she again asked for a song, big Barreau,

who had slain his thousands of trees, and rafted innumerable drams down the rapids, for the first time volunteered a song. He commenced :

> " Nous avons sauté le Long Sault,
>   Nous l'avons sauté tout d'un morceau.
>   Ah ! que l'hiver est long !
>   Dans les chantiers nous hivernerons,
>   Dans les chantiers nous hivernerons !"

but fell back, blushing violently, after racking his memory in vain for the words of the second verse.

When the drams were moored in safety at Smart's Bay (opposite Cornwall), that Friday night, an oar was laid between the dram and the shore as a sort of "gang-plank." It is scarcely necessary to say that those who wished to go ashore dry had to do some nice feats of balancing. The little lady and her papa were taking leave of us. Papa performed on that oar like an elephant on a tight rope, and would in all probability have got wet had he not beat a hasty retreat. At these demonstrations of papa's the little lady laughed very undutifully and declared her intention of "going first." The words were scarcely uttered before there was a splash heard, and the little lady was carried ashore, like a child, in the brawny arms of a six-foot raftsman who found no difficulty in walking through four feet of water, even with her as a load. She doubtless was a little startled, but the gallant fellow meant well, and his act was a farewell tribute to her pluck.

Before eleven o'clock next morning the drams were lashed together; then set out for Coteau with a steam-tug at their head. The procession moved solemnly through

Lake St. Francis, the monotony being broken only by
passing steamboats, propellers or grain barges, whose
passengers eyed us with an interest which was flattering.
Perhaps some of them regarded us as on our way to de-
struction, and shed pitying tears.   We certainly grieved
for their captivity, though we too were " cribbed, cabined
and confined."   It is not pleasant sometimes to be an object of interest ; but on a raft one learns to endure with
patience even a stare through a field-glass.   When we
were glared at by lady passengers on the steamboats,
even the most sunburnt of us showed a heightened colour.
By this time constant exposure had blackened some com-
plexions, and given to others a scarlet hue whose brilli-
ancy almost answered the purpose of flint and steel at
night.   Bardolph's nose was not a circumstance to noses
on board.   More than one person might have had applied
to him, with appropriateness, Falstaff's apostrophe to his
famous swash-buckler: "Thou art the Knight of the Burn-
ing Lamp."   But as all were more or less sun-painted—com-
plexion veils being out of the question—there was little
comparison of hues.   Like ladies at a ball or an opera, we
by common consent tabooed the subject.   At seven in the
evening our destination was reached, and, as the French
raftsmen whose assistance was required for the next
rapids would not run them on Sunday, we spent that day
in the village.   At five next morning we found the raft
fairly alive with men.   There were ten drams, and each
dram took about seventeen additional hands and a pilot
to work through, at a cost of about $2.50 per man, and
$6.00 to the pilot.   According as the drams were unfast-
ened they moved off, the big sweeps making not unpleas-

ant music as they struck the water in steady unison.
The bell of the village church rang out a parting blessing.
The men crossed themselves and knelt for a few moments
to pray for a safe journey ; and the women and children
on shore waived adieux to their fathers, husbands, broth-
ers, and lovers—for certainly it seemed that we had
carried away the entire male population of the pleasantly
situated but exceedingly quiet village. The Coteau and
the Cedars (about nine miles apart) were taken at the
rate of twelve miles an hour, with the loss of a few sticks
of timber, which were driven out of the bottom of the
dram as it bounded over a huge boulder, and plunged its
bow too deep into the water. One unlucky dram immediately behind us, had entered the rapid sideways, and
being caught in an eddy, whirled and twirled its huge
length around until its helpless gyrations almost dizzied
those who watched it. Tired with its plaything, the
current at last shot it high and dry on shore at a safe
but puzzling spot, where its crew had to work at the unsatisfactory task of re-rafting. Five miles further on, the
Cascades were encountered, with the well-known Split
Rock guarding the entrance like a granite Cerberus. The
dangers of the rapids are lost sight of by a tourist on a
steamboat ; to appreciate them one must, as it were,
mingle in the fray, feel on his cheek the foam cast up by
the seething waters around him, have his ears filled with
their din, and his eyes startled by the rock apparitions
which emerge and disappear in an instant, like porpoises
at play. The Ile des Cascades lies a short distance from
the Pointe des Cascades and, with two or three other
smaller islands, breaks the current of the river at its en-

trance into Lake St. Louis. Here the drams shoot into
the whirl of waters produced by a sudden declivity in
the river, whose bed is obstructed by rocks in some
places, and scooped into cavities in others. The bow
oarsmen receive the first shower-bath with resolution,
but on the approach of a dense mass of upreared water,
rush to the middle of the dram to avoid the onset. Too
late! they are knocked down like ten-pins, and left
(luckily for them) sprawling in all directions on the
sticks of timber, to which they cling with the tenacity
of barnacles. Though rocking like a cradle our good
ship rises and plunges forward with desperate energy
and equal strength, and gains headway again in the current. A feeling of awe comes over one, gazing thus upon
the contest. The descending waters are precipitated
with great velocity between the islands, repelled with
seemingly an equal force by the rocks and hollows underneath, then thrown up in spherical figures high above the
surface, and driven back once more upon the current.
Through this tempest the pilot guides his unwieldy
charge, skimming shoals which seemingly block all entrance, and, by a skilful and swift turn, grazing reefs
which are apparently unavoidable at our headlong speed.
Once more we are through in safety, and in Lake St.
Louis have a little leisure to think of absent friends. Soon
they come along one after another, but "not the six
hundred;" instead of nine, only seven put in an appearance, and we hear with selfish complacency that one is
aground and the other "absent without leave," no one
knows why. But as the rule is every one for himself, we
proceed on our way towards Nun's Island, having first

disembarked the Coteau oarsmen.   A steam-tug awaited
our arrival at the foot of the rapids and took us in tow.
While going through the lake we learned that the Beau-
harnois canal, 11½ miles long, built to avoid these three
rapids, has a rise of lockage of 82½ feet.   Six o'clock in
the evening found us at anchor near Chateauguay.

The last rapid was to be run on the morrow, and, the
night being before us, a little relaxation was indulged in.
Visitors from the shore came aboard in canoes, and we
were soon on speaking terms with the civilized descendants of the Caughnawaga Indians.   Theirs was not a
visit of ceremony; they meant business.   The Lachine
could not be run without their assistance.   The foreman
of the raft gave audience to the most Indian-looking of
the visitors, and after a brief pow-wow, we learned that
a selection of pilots and oarsmen had been made.   Each
pilot has his gang of men who accompany him on every
voyage down, and by arrangement with him their services are secured.   The wages given are $2½ per man, $8
or $10 apiece to the pilot and sub-pilots.   These wages
are earned only when the drams are moored in safety at
Montreal; when a dram is wrecked no one gets paid ;
when put on a shoal, the crew work away until it is
taken off, no matter how many days, and receive no further pay than if the usual time were consumed.   So "no
success, no pay" is the rule of the river adopted to secure
due precaution and skill in pilotage.   There is no hig-
gling over wages.   Custom has laid down a tariff, and
none expect more or will take less than the usual fees.
In a very short time, therefore, everything is arranged,
and the Indians depart as silently as they came, with

strict orders to be on board at three o'clock next morning. The raftsmen huddle together in the shanties, the
fires are stirred up, and cards, dancing, jokes, stories, and
songs find their place in the programme of the night.
The tourists are told that the most dangerous rapid, the
Lachine, has yet to be run, and are plied with tales of
hair-breadth escapes from drowning; of drams that had
broken from their mooring at night in a gale, and had
shot the rapids without pilotage; of drams that had struck
rocks in such a manner as to cause the sticks of timber
to bounce up high in the air; of drams that had
been sucked into eddies and had bathed their crews in
six or seven feet of water; of drams that had gone to
pieces, and whose unleashed logs had jammed and pounded
every one on board into unrecognizable pulp—in fact all
the rafting horrors of years are renewed for the especial
benefit of the laymen whose fortune it is to be present
at the night's recital. But no terror was equal to the
ridicule which would have been ours had we gone ashore
on the eve of the event which was to cap the climax of
the voyage; or to the contempt which would have rendered our names immortally luminous in raftsman's story
had we yielded to the promptings of an unbiassed discre-
tion; so, looking as cheerful as possible, we stowed away
a more than liberal allowance of hard-tack, potatoes and
tea, and contributed a fair share of the heroic to the
night's entertainment. Martyrs to rashness, we could
not help endeavouring to recall the particulars of our
life policies, so spent a moment or two in wondering
whether the suicide clause applied to rapids. But the
1st Clown in Hamlet, act V., sc. 1, reassured us: " If the

man go to this water and drown himself, it is will-he,
nill-he, he goes; mark you that? but if the water come
to him, and drown him, he drowns not himself: Argal,
he that is not guilty of his own death, shortens not his
own life." This train of thought was consoling, and to
the surprise of many, one of us without invitation or
pressure announced himself as a volunteer songster. His
song was "The night before Larry was stretched." It
was too lugubrious, so another broke in with—

"Malbrough s'en va-t-en guerre,
    Mironton, mironton, mirontaine;
Malbrough s'en va-t-en guerre,
    Ne sait quand reviendra."

This was too suggestive; but the unexpected display
of temerity, as may be supposed, raised the tone of the
meeting, and a refrain, thrilling, though scarcely intelligible, followed:—

"C'était un vieux sauvage,
Tout noir, tout barbouillé,
    Ouick' ka!

Avec sa vieille couverte,
Et son sac à tabac,
    Ouick' ka!

Ah! ah! tenaouich' tenaga
Tenaouich' tenaga, ouick' ka!"

The neighbourhood being full of legend, it was to be
expected that a little prompting would draw out some
story-teller. An attempt was only too successful. Jean
Baptiste (it is as thick here as Jones or Brown elsewhere)
remembered, at great length, that his grandfather had
rescued from the Lachine a young Indian warrior and an

M

Indian maid, the course of whose love had been as obstructed as the channel through the rapid. The lovers
had walked into the river, one frosty morning, hand in
hand, intending to drown in each others' arms, but the
aforesaid grandfather being lynx-eyed and an early riser,
discovered them before they had got far into the stream,
and brought them out by raising his gun to his shoulder,
and threatening to riddle them with buck-shot. They returned sadly to the shore. The warrior shot himself next
day, but the maiden, grieved to the heart at his folly,
lived on for many years which she improved by becoming an expert hand at a raft oar, and earning large wages
in the rapid. The romance has never been done into
verse, so ballad writers may, with impunity, make use of
the melancholy particulars. What confirms one's belief
in the truthfulness of the story is the fact that a few
years ago, when men were scarce hereabouts, women's
rights so far as work was concerned being recognized,
squaws were hired to assist at the oars, two of them
being considered equal to one man. The love story had
the effect of turning the channel of song from the heroic
to the sentimental, and the young man Henri trolled out
lustily :

> " Vive la Canadienne,
>   Vole, mon cœur vole,
> Vive la Canadienne,
>   Et ses jolis yeux doux,
> Et ses jolis yeux doux, tous doux,
>   Et ses jolis yeux doux.
>
> " Nous la menons aux noces,
>   Vole, mon cœur vole,
> Nous la menons aux noces,
>   Dans tous ses beaux atours."

This was too much for the cook, who declared that if the entertainment was to last all night, supper might be indulged in with recklessness.   His remarks were loudly cheered, and by way of response he brought in supper in his arms, that is to say, he dived into the hard-tack barrel, and cast upon the table large supplies of biscuit rigid enough to make any teeth, save those of a raftsman, water.   False teeth would never serve a useful purpose on a raft.   But hard-tack goes very fairly, if well-soaked, and the eater has in its favour the prejudice acquired by long abstinence from anything else.   It economises time also, which is of some importance on board a raft, as it obviates the conventional objection to a person going about with his meals in his pocket.   By way of dessert the cook treated us to some raspberries and raw onions, which he had received from a squaw the day before, in exchange for grease.   After this prosaic interruption of the feast of reason, which had characterized the night, it was deemed best for all to go to sleep.   Ten minutes after the advice had been given all hands were snoring. At three in the morning the Indians came on board, according to orders, and by six everything had been got ready, and the drams cleared for the run.   Twenty-six men rowed on each.   The sun was shining out gloriously ; not a breath of wind stirred the surface of the river.   The oars swung in their holders with a uniform thud.   The men pulled, of course, standing up, and as they were on the lowest tier or bottom of the dram, they moved constantly in five or six inches of water.   However, damp feet are not a cause of anxiety to a raftsman.   Between Lachine and Caughnawaga the breadth of the St. Law-

rence narrows to about half a mile. As we pass the
churches on either shore, the men drop on their knees
and say their prayers—some for a moment or two, others
for a longer time. There is little or no noise save the
splash of oars, and there is much less profanity than is
usually heard. "Don't swear till we get through the
Lachine," says one rebukingly to an irate companion.
The roar of the rapid is now heard. The pace is getting
faster and faster every instant. The drams stretch out
in line of battle, and the pilot's voice is more frequently
heard shouting his orders: "En haut," meaning row
away at the bow; "à derrière," at the stern. Now, the
bow oars are alone at work; now, the men at the stern
make their oars bend with a will; now all, at bow, stern
and sides, pull with their utmost strength. Everything
depends on how and where we enter the rapids, and as
the pilot mops his brow with his red handkerchief, we
know that the time has come for all his presence of mind,
all his skill. A few feet to the wrong side may suffice to
cause him the loss of his pay, and ourselves the loss of
our lives. From Caughnawaga to the lower extremity
of the rapid, a distance of nearly four miles, there is a
gradual shelving descent of the rocky bed of the river.
The stream in passing down acquires an irresistible impetus, and towards the lower part runs with a velocity of
eighteen miles an hour, until it is separated by some
islands below into several channels. Into this ravine we
glide with tremendous rapidity, and take the first pitch
like a cork, all hands seeking a dry spot in the middle of
the dram, until a heavy wave strikes and passes over.
Straight onward the dram speeds, the men giving their

whole strength to their oars to keep it in the proper course. Now a corner is to be turned, and the violence of the waters is such that the men in the bow can with difficulty retain their places. There is a very Babel of voices. The pilot, notwithstanding his Indian blood, springs to and fro on the timber, and shouts excitedly to the men in a mixture of Indian and French, and the sturdy fellows yell encouragement to each other, with savage appreciation of the danger. Wave after wave gathers itself in a mass and tumbles on us as if seeking to conquer by sheer weight of water; wave after wave dashes itself to fragments against our sturdy side. The shanty leaps into the air; over goes the stove; down come the stove-pipes; the withes can almost be heard to shriek with the agony of extreme tension, and the sticks of timber move restlessly in their faithful clutch. The excitement culminates in a roar of triumph, as the drams swing round the point of danger and cleave the waves with a hissing sound which tells how fearful is the speed. The men again leap to their oars. In a moment or two we have passed through a stretch of comparative calm; shot over a rocky ledge on the crests of billows so much engaged in smashing each other as to be careless of the use to which they were put by us; and gone headlong down the third pitch. The dram emerges spluttering, and shakes its high sides like a Newfoundland dog. The men are again at their posts, dripping but joyful, and the pilot stands quietly mopping huge patches of perspiration from his face. "A pretty rough passage, pilot," one ventures to observe. "The best I have had, Sir; you brought luck with you." The Victoria Bridge was now

in sight, and after passing underneath one of its spans,
we were, about two o'clock, brought to anchor near Montreal.   Some of the drams which came out of the rapid
too far to the south, found themselves carried by the current on shoals, where they were forced to lie until towed
off by steamboats.   A good many sticks of timber were
floating about, which men in canoes rescued and delivered
up on payment of fifty cents a stick for salvage.   These
men are called " Le gang quarante," or the Forty Thieves,
as their honesty in returning lost timber is questionable.   Next day the raft started for Quebec in charge of
a steam-tug.   As the three days' voyage down was somewhat monotonous, and as the reader is by this time familiar with, if not tired of, life on a raft, it will suffice to
add that for generosity, profanity, recklessness, industry,
kindness, courage, endurance and simple mindedness,
mingled in an olla podrida of manhood, no class will compare with the stalwart, swarthy fellows who annually
take our timber to the sea.

THE LATE ADAM CLARKE TYNER

[Mr. Foster in the *Daily Telegraph*.]

———— •✦• ————

W E have a duty to perform, as well to the dead as to the living, and we halt, even amid the excitement and agitation of a crisis of affairs, to lay our chaplet on the bier of one who, gifted beyond his fellows, won an enviable place in public esteem. The announcement made yesterday that Adam Clarke Tyner had yielded up his young life brought a pang to many a heart and, though the event was not unexpected, the shock was none the less painful. We scarcely know how to discharge our duty aright. His name, wherever spoken, carries with it its own eulogy, for none knew him who did not yield a willing homage to his ability, none enjoyed his friendship who did not cherish it as a boon, precious and pure.

No panegyric of ours can add to the memory of our departed friend and associate. But his genial presence, his flashing wit, his goodness of heart, his lavish generosity, his tenderness, his modesty, all come back to us with a vividness of recollection that shows only too clearly the magnitude of our loss, and makes us painfully conscious how strong was his hold on our affection. The felicities of his life renew themselves in all their exquisite minuteness, and we hesitate to give voice to the many thoughts that seek expression in the language of friendship. Few were so gifted as he who has passed from our midst, few had a brighter future, and none bore well-won honours with more meekness. Pretence was foreign to his nature; his heart was too large for meanness. Many of our readers will recollect his reading of the "May Queen," and as they pay the last sad tribute to departed worth, they can easily recall his pathetic tones, telling of one who had gone—

> "Where the wicked cease from troubling,
> And the weary are at rest."

IN MEMORIAM.

TRIBUTES CALLED FORTH BY MR. FOSTER'S DEATH.

THE LATE WILLIAM ALEXANDER FOSTER, Q.C

BY MR. G. MERCER ADAM, TORONTO.

[From *The Week*, Nov. 8th, 1888.]

"THERE are few heroes in our Pantheon," is an observation made by the subject of this brief sketch, in his ringing, national address on "Canada First," delivered now almost twenty years ago. "Where every man does his duty," adds Mr. Foster, "heroes are not wanted and are not missed." At the grave of one who eminently though unostentatiously did his duty, and who in doing it so well sadly shortened his active, useful life, these wise, sane words, if recalled at all, must have come home with impressive force to the hearts of all who knew him who uttered them. The age is too commonplace and the pursuits of the time are too unromantic for heroes. Yet if we cannot call him a hero who honestly and earnestly does his duty and lives a true, honourable and unselfish life, the few, at least, to whom such a one is known feel how allied well-performed duty is to heroism, and how great is the wrench when they have to part with one whose brief life was distinguished by those qualities. The memory preserved in the public heart of the best that ever lived, we know, is comparatively short; but short as it is, it cannot with truth be said that a good and useful life counts for little, or that, by its contemporaries at least, such a life will not be missed. After one is gone, the perspective of the passing years is often cruel to individual memory. That the memory of Mr. Foster, with the recollection of his fine professional career and high personal qualities, will be kept longer green than is the meed of thousands, we do not say. But this we say, that before the influence and impress of his character have faded, and before regard for him as a friend has died out from the hearts of those who knew and loved him, Time will have taken hence most of those who were his contemporaries.

It would be foolish to claim for Mr. Foster a position far above the average of his fellows. As a professional man he had many and uncommon gifts. He was shrewd and clear-sighted in counsel and apt and skilful in the management of cases in court. He was moreover, an indefatigable, though not always a ready, worker. He was painstaking in all that he undertook, straightforward in his dealings, courteous to all with whom he came in contact, and possessed a largeness of soul and a geniality of disposition that endeared him to thousands. That he spared himself in nothing, his devotion to business, and the strain he suffered himself to endure before his weakened frame and shattered nervous system broke under the load, sufficiently attest.

It was in his early days, however, and as an aspirant
for literary and political, rather than for legal and forensic fame, that the writer of this knew him best. When
we first met, he had graduated at his *Alma Mater*, and,
like many of his young associates, not a few of whom,
alas! have preceded him to the tomb, he had qualified
himself to follow law as a profession. Notwithstanding
this fact we found him much drawn to literature, for the
pursuit of which he had marked gifts, and, like some of
his colleg econtemporaries, had a strong mental bias. Pol-
itically, the times were favourable for a young man of
ardent temperament as well as of acknowledged ability
to make his mark in literature. Compelled to seek a way
out of the party deadlock of the time, the country had
just committed itself to the experiment of Confederation.
A new and higher national life opened before the people.
Many of the political leaders were journalistic athletes,
and some of them at least—like Cartier, Howe and Mc-
Gee—were in sympathy with literature. Under the in-
influence of these—especially of the ill-fated McGee—
literary enterprise, for a time at any rate, felt the glow of
national inspiration and the quickening of a new birth.
Of those to feel the effect of the new awakening, young
Foster, as the most fervent, was the first. Besides his
overflowing patriotism, he had added to his natural gifts
facility in literary composition, and had already published an article in the London *Westminster* on " Canadian
Nationality." This he followed by his lecture on " Canada
First," an eloquent and inspiring resumé of Canadian
achievement. Others catching his enthusiasm, " Canada
First" soon became a rallying cry to the youth of the bud-

ding nation, and the next step was the organization of a party with the rousing watchword on its banners.   Space here forbids us from following the fortunes of this nationalist party.   Its vicissitudes, however, are well known ; and though it accomplished little in practical politics— partly because of journalistic and party jealousy, and partly because the people had had enough of the political ailments of the time—it awakened youthful desire for intellectual freedom and for an increased measure of political independence.   In this good work it was fortunate in winning the advocacy of an able and brilliant pen, till then new to the country, which, heedless of abuse and obloquy, was trenchantly wielded in the cause which the young patriots had at heart.   With amazing public ingratitude and inconsistency this writer, forgetful of what he has all along done for the best interests of Canada, is to-day called disloyal, and accused of burrowing beneath the feet of the nation.   The trouble with this charge is that the nation is still but a colony and has never yet got upon its feet.   Not the least of the valuable results of the " Canada First" movement were the founding and the maintenance for a while, of *The Nation* and *The Canadian Monthly*, and the erection in Toronto of the National Club.

But the movement into which Mr. Foster and his friends enthusiastically threw themselves was, as we know, short-lived. Canadian patriotism was fatally handicapped by Party, and Party neither looked then, nor does it look now, to higher ends than its own ignoble interests. Since that period, the fibre of Canadian nationality has, we fear relaxed instead of hardened, and the aspirations born of

the time have, in the main, vanished into thin air.   For
this Mr. Foster was in no way responsible, for, with the
ardour and persistence of youth, he clung to the movement until he and his allies were accused of tilting at
windmills and of "dreaming dreams." Though loth to accept
discomfiture, Mr. Foster could not fail, however, to realize
facts, and he now turned aside to take up his profession,
In law he found, if not the pursuit on which his heart was
set, that which pecuniarily was more to his interest. With
the exception of occasional contributions to journalism,
literature he now and forever forsook.   In this, from a
worldly point of view, he no doubt did wisely; though
had he followed letters as a means of livelihood and prac-
tised it where it is recognized and rewarded as a profession, he would have won, we feel sure, both fortune and
fame.   To these allurements, and to everything earthly,
his eyes and ears, alas! are now dull.   The familiar figure
of our friend is to us now but a memory.   It is a memory,
however, that we would fain cherish, for, as with all who
knew his worth, we esteemed him and gave him our
heart.   At his grave, where his remains were paid the
honours due to a beloved friend, his fellow-townsmen took
leave not only of a good citizen but of a true patriot.

MR. FOSTER'S CAREER REVIEWED.

BY MR. HENRY J. MORGAN, OTTAWA.

[From the *Ottawa Citizen*, Nov. 6th, 1888.]

Another professional man has fallen a victim to overwork, in the person of the eminent barrister whose name
heads this article, and whose sudden death towards the
close of last week, before he had reached his 49th year,
has occasioned more than ordinary regret throughout the
Province.   As solicitor to the liquidators in the settlement of the affairs of the unfortunate Central Bank, the
late Mr. Foster had for some considerable time devoted
himself with extraordinary zeal and uncommon ability
to the disentangling of the financial labyrinth before him.
It was truly a herculean task, the performance of which
taxed the physical and mental energies of the lamented
gentleman to the very utmost.   It is stated that he gave
not only his days but his nights also to the exacting and
fatiguing labour, taking no rest or recreation,—all this
continuing day after day and month after month for upwards of a year.   No one of ordinary fibre could long
endure so severe a strain, and, as could easily have been
foreseen, Mr. Foster's physical powers at length gave way.
But he still continued at his post, and it was only when
overborne by disease—the result of a cold contracted in
the execution of his duties—that he resigned into other
hands the task he had hoped himself to achieve.   Rarely
have we been called upon to chronicle a display of devotion so entirely unselfish at the shrine of duty.   The sud-

den and untimely removal of one of Mr. Foster's prominence and usefulness, both as a professional man and a
private citizen, and the causes which have contributed
to that unfortunate event, inculcate a lesson which our
professional and public men would do well to ponder and
take to heart. There is too much work and too little
play in this restless and pushing generation. The late
Mr. Foster, in addition to a distinguished place at the
Bar, had won a high position as a literary man. While
yet a student at the University of Toronto (of whose
Senate he in after years became a member), he, together
with the late Thomas Moss, subsequently Chief Justice
of Ontario, W. J. Rattray, author of the SCOT IN CANADA,
and others, contributed largely to a humorous weekly
called the GRUMBLER, published in Toronto by Erastus
Wiman, the now famous capitalist of New York. At a
later period he was a contributor to the editorial columns
of the Toronto LEADER, the Hamilton SPECTATOR and the
Toronto TELEGRAPH. He was also for a considerable
period chief editor of the MONETARY TIMES. When the
project for a Confederation of the B. N. A. Provinces
came before the people, Mr. Foster wrote an exceedingly
able paper on the subject for the WESTMINSTER REVIEW,
and subsequently, contributed a second article on " Confederation and Reciprocity " to the same periodical. In
both articles he warmly supported the scheme of union,
as submitted to Parliament by Sir John Macdonald. He
also favoured a renewal of the old Reciprocity Treaty,
negotiated by Lord Elgin. Other contributions from his
pen on Canadian affairs appeared in the London SPEC-
TATOR, the London ATHENÆUM and the London TIMES,
and for some years he was the Canadian correspondent

of the latter paper. If we mistake not, he also wrote
occasionally for THE NATION and the CANADIAN MONTH-
LY.   His contributions to periodical and newspaper
literature covered a wide range of subjects, chiefly, however, relating to domestic politics and questions of Imperial Colonial policy.   Like Thomas D'Arcy McGee and
other great minds, he was a sincere believer in the future
destiny of Canada as a distinct nationality, and lost no
opportunity of preaching this doctrine in season and out
of season. This belief—it might almost be called a religion
with him—found notable and eloquent utterance in his
well-known essay entitled " CANADA FIRST ; OR, A NEW
NATIONALITY," which was published in pamphlet form
shortly after the Red River insurrection of 1869, a work
much admired by the young Ontarians of the day for its
lofty tone and patriotic sentiment. The publication of
this essay led to the formation of what was known as the
" Canada First" party, of which Mr. Foster was the
acknowledged leader, and among whose members were
many young Canadians who have since attained distinction in their walks of life, William H. Howland, late
Mayor of Toronto ; George T. Denison, now Police Magis-
trate of Toronto ; Joseph Easton Macdougall, now Judge
of York ; Charles Mair, the author of " Tecumseh ;" John
Schultz, now Lieutenant-Governor of Manitoba ; Robert
Grant Haliburton, the scientist and littérateur ; Frederick C. Denison, C.M.G., now M. P. for West Toronto ;
William B. McMurrich, late Mayor of Toronto ; James H.
Morris, Q. C., and Hugh Scott, insurance agent, being of
the number. The party controlled one or two organs of
public opinion and erected a club house—the National—
which became the rallying-place of " Canada First" ad-

herents and disciples living in and visiting the Ontario capital. "Canada First," however, ceased to exist, as a separate organization, with the birth of the National Policy in 1878—a policy which, as our readers all know, became the main plank in the political platform of the party of Union and Progress (now the Liberal Conservative party), under the leadership of Sir John Macdonald and which policy carried the Conservatives to victory at the polls on the 17th of September of the year above mentioned. From that time Mr. Foster devoted himself almost exclusively to his law business, and some years since obtained a silk gown from the present Government in recognition of his legal talent. Had he been spared to his country a few years longer, we think there cannot be any doubt of his succeeding to higher rewards in a profession of which he was for many years so distinguished an ornament. It must, despite his untimely demise, be a great consolation to Mr. Foster's family and friends to reflect that he died nobly in the discharge of duty. Many of the world's greatest workers and best men have thus died in harness, and have even wished that it might be so. "Much better to die doing," was a favourite saying with Charles Dickens. Mr. Foster was emphatically a man of the militant type, in the best sense of that qualification, a soldier of what he conceived to be the Right. It is rarely indeed that we can look back on a record so symmetrical in all its relations—so flawless and unimpeachable. "Well done good and faithful servant," will, we feel sure, be the sentence uttered to this valiant soldier of duty by the great Captain and Lord of Hosts when He shall call the rolls at the Last Day.

N

IN MEMORY OF WILLIAM A. FOSTER.

———

By Mr. CHARLES MAIR, PRINCE ALBERT, N.W.T.

[From *The Week*, February 1st, 1889.]

AND he is gone, who led the few
  Forecasters of a nation fair ;
That gentle spirit, strong and true,
  As ever breathed Canadian air!

Forever fled ! the kindly face,
  The eager look, the lambent eye,
Still haunted by a boyish grace—
  Can these from recollection fly ?

The counsel sound, the judgment clear,
  The mild thought brooding over all,
The ready smile, the ready tear—
  Can these from recollection fall ?

Ah ! well do I remember still
  The sultry day whose sun had set ;
The hostel near the tower-crowned hill,*
  The parlour dim where first we met ;

The quickened hope, the joy divine,
  On that pale eve of loftier times,†
When, with his friendly hand in mine,
  He praised my poor Canadian rhymes ;

And sung the old Canadian songs,§
  And played the old Canadian airs,
Then turned his smile on fancied wrongs,
  And laughed away a youth's despairs ;

---

* Parliament Hill. † Confederation. ‡ Mr. Foster was fond of French-
Canadian song ; its vivacity and plaintiveness equally touched him.

And said : " Throw sickly thoughts aside—
   Let's build on native fields our fame ;
Nor seek to blend our patriot pride
   With alien worth, or alien shame !

" Nor trust the falterers who despond—
   The doubting spirits which divine
No stable future save beyond
   Their long, imaginary line !

" But mark, by fate's strong finger traced
   Our country's rise ; see time unfold,
In our own land, a nation based
   On manly deeds, not lust for gold.

" Its bourne, the home of generous life,
   Of ample freedom, slowly won,
Of modest maid and faithful wife,
   Of simple love 'twixt sire and son.

" Nor lessened would the duty be
   To rally, then, around the throne ;
A filial nation, strong and free—
   Great Britain's child to manhood grown !

" But lift the curtain which deceives,
   The veil that intercepts the sight,
The drapery dependence weaves
   To screen us from the nobler light.

" First feel throughout the throbbing land
   A nation's pulse, a nation's pride ;
The independent life—then stand
   Erect, unbound, at Britain's side ! "

And many a year has fled and now
   The tongue which voiced the thought is stilled ;
The veil yet hangs o'er many a brow,
   The glorious dream is unfulfilled.

Yet ocean unto ocean cries !
  For us their mighty tides go forth.
We front the sun, behind us lies
  The mystery of the unconquered North !

And ardent Aspiration peers
  Beyond the clouds, beyond the night,
Beyond the faltering, paltering years,
  And there beholds the breaking light !

For though the thoughtful mind has passed
  From mortal ken, the generous hand—
The seed they sowed has sprung at last,
  And grows and blossoms through the laud.

And time will realise the dream,
  The light yet spread o'er land and wave ;
And Honour, in that hour supreme,
  Will hang his wreath o'er Foster's grave.

TRIBUTES FROM THE TORONTO PRESS.

The *Mail* (Nov. 2, 1888).

It will be learned with profound regret that Mr. W. A. Foster, the widely known lawyer, is dead.   *   *   *
Early in life he manifested a fancy for literary pursuits, and the gifts which promised for him an entirely successful career. There is little doubt that had he adopted literature exclusively he would have made as high a reputation for himself as he enjoyed in the legal profession.   *   *   *

Those who knew Mr. Foster personally, and were therefore acquainted with his many good qualities and virtues, will feel sincerely sorry to hear of his death. Those who knew him only by reputation will recognize the fact that an exceedingly able man had passed away. He was entirely devoted to his profession, and followed it with even too great an ardour. The interests of his clients were ever sacred to him, and his duties to men were always fully and faithfully performed.

The *Mail* (Nov. 5th, 1888).

Around a newly excavated grave in the Necropolis there gathered on Saturday a sorrowful circle of Toronto's most worthy citizens, to commit to their last resting-place the mortal remains of one who was almost universally loved and respected. As the sound of falling sand indicated that Wm. A. Foster was being entombed in the bosom of Mother Earth, many eyes wet with tears told how hard had been the severance of mutual ties of friendship. The funeral of the late Mr. Foster was especially solemn and impressive. To many he had been endeared by his amiable and unpretentious life. To others his self-sacrificing devotion to duty had been a source of respect and admiration. To all with whom he came in contact he was a friend. Among those who attended the last services were leading jurists of Ontario, distinguished members of the bar, clergymen of several denominations, and business men of high standing. The gathering was alike a tribute of respect for the deceased and an expression of sympathy for the bereaved family

The time appointed for the funeral was three o'clock. As the hour approached, the friends of the deceased, began to assemble to pay the last tribute of respect to his memory. The house could not contain them, and one by one, after a last look at the calm features of the deceased, they gathered in groups outside on the lawn and discussed the deceased's merits and extolled his virtues. Upon no other occasion could such a gathering of men, leaders on the bench, at the bar, in literature, art, religion and science in this Dominion be brought together, an expressive tribute to the sterling qualities of him who lay so cold and still in an inner room.   *   *   *   *

The funeral services were conducted by the Rev. Coverdale Watson, pastor of the Central Methodist Church, assisted by the Rev. Drs. Dewart, Johnston, and Potts.

The pall-bearers were all intimate friends of the deceased, some of them associates in the Canada First movement.   They were: The Hon. Mr. Justice Osler, the Hon. Mr. Justice Falconbridge, Mr. Wm. H. Howland, Lieut.-Col. Geo. T. Denison, Mr. C. W. Bunting, Mr. Hugh Scott, Mr. Charles Moss, Q.C., and Mr. John Ross Robertson.

The *Globe* (Nov. 2nd, 1888).

In his profession, Mr. Foster has long been regarded as one of the most painstaking members of the Bar.   He was always thorough in preparing his case, taking home his work and sitting up till long after midnight preparing his brief. In giving his opinion on any technical point, he devoted such earnest thought to the subject as to secure from his brethren their entire confidence in his decision. * * *

Mr. Foster was one of the brightest of the band of clever and enthusiastic young men who conducted the "Canada First" agitation between fifteen and twenty years ago. * * *

In the early days of his legal career, Mr. Foster gave considerable attention to newspaper and magazine writing, and in this department showed marked proficiency. * * *

The *Empire* (Nov. 3, 1888).

The news of the death of W. A. Foster, Q. C., was the chief topic of conversation yesterday in all circles, and never was more genuine regard expressed than was to be heard on every hand. At Osgoode Hall, and in the lawyers' offices especially, the great abilities and the many good qualities of the deceased were the theme. * * * Sorrow was depicted on the countenances of Judge McDougall and the lawyers who attended the County Court yesterday. They mourned the sudden taking off of their worthy friend, W. A. Foster, Q. C., who died on Thursday night. Judge McDougall spoke feelingly of the loss which the profession had sustained in the death of Mr. Foster, who had been a prominent and respected member of the Bar, and a man who stood high in the estimation of all who knew him.

The *World* (Nov. 2nd, 1888).

During the whole course of his legal practice he was noted for his devotion to his profession, and to the interests of his clients. At the time of his death he was one of the most prominent counsel at the Ontario Bar.

While yet a student he developed a fine literary taste. *   *   * He was the author of the article entitled "Canada First," which gave that name a prominence and influence lasting up to the present time. The deceased gentleman was one of the founders and sole editor of the *Monetary Times* during its early days. He might, had he attended to it exclusively, have achieved as great a success in literature as in law.   *   *   * His genial disposition and great talents endeared him to all who knew him either in his professional or social capacity.   *   *   *

He had a wonderful grasp of the facts of each case, and in the course of his duties he subjected witnesses to some of the keenest cross-examinations which have taken place in Osgoode Hall. In his longer addresses to the court, whether in stating the case of the bank or analysing and replying to the speeches of counsel on the other side, he occasionally rose to flights of forensic eloquence. But he was a straight and fair hitter, and no blows were dealt "below the belt." On the eve of the long vacation, Master Hodgins paid a high tribute to the zeal, ability and fair mindedness of the deceased counsel. The other counsel, whose name is legion, applauded this sentiment and personally paid deserved encomiums to Mr. Foster.   *   * In his lamented death the legal fraternity of Toronto is bereft of one who was universally liked for his sterling qualities of head and heart, who was a true friend, a genial companion, and who sought to elevate his profession and his numerous co-workers.

The *World* (Nov. 5, 1888).

Seldom of recent years has any citizen had such an honored funeral as that of Mr. W. A. Foster, Q.C., on Saturday afternoon. Universally respected by the citizens generally, beloved by those who lament his sterling worth, a man with "troops of friends" and never an enemy, all classes of society were present to pay their tribute to his memory. The Bench, the Bar, the legal societies, the ministers of all denominations, City Fathers, distinguished professors, and a legion of friends and neighbours took their last fond look of the well-known features so calm in death.

Toronto Daily News (Nov. 2, 1888).

It is with deep regret that The *News* chronicles the death of Mr. W. A. Foster, Q.C., as worthy a man and as able a lawyer as it has been its good fortune to know. Clever in his profession, high in the esteem of those who knew him, and loved and respected by all who were acquainted with the high qualities of his mind, he leaves a gap in professional and social ranks which will not easily be filled. Perhaps the most amiable trait of his generous character was his loyalty to Canada and things Canadian, which was a principle with him, striven for, warmly advocated and deeply revered. But being of a retiring disposition, and indifferent to the honours or attractions of being in the lead, he held himself aloof from the wrangle of party politics, and only ventured into

them when they bore upon the subject which he had
deeply at heart, Canadian nationality.   *   *   *

The *Telegram* (Nov. 2, 1888).

"A GOOD CANADIAN GONE."

The untimely death of W. A. Foster, Q.C., is a loss to
the country, the city, and above all, to his bereaved friends
and family.

To his country, because he loved it. He was a Canadian. With the eye of a patriot, he was among the first
to see the rock ahead of this Dominion. His voice and
pen warned his countrymen against those enemies of
national life—the strife of parties and the bitterness
between provinces that are still corroding the soul of
Canada.

Toronto loses in him one who was emphatically a good
citizen. A retiring disposition and the demands of his
profession kept Mr. Foster from prominently identifying
himself with movements calculated to advance its material interests. In their success he ever had the keenest
interest, and many workers for the good of his native
city found in him a friend.

But the sorrow falls most heavily upon the hearts of
those who knew him best. To the many he was known
as an honest, able, fearless lawyer. To the few he was
the friend whose friendship changed not with the years.
They mourn for the modest, genial, kindly man who has
so soon gone home. And sympathy for the household in
mourning speaks in the sorrow of all who knew William
A. Foster.

The Christian Guardian (Nov. 7th, 1888).

The sudden death of W. A. Foster, Q.C., the well-known barrister and literary writer of this city, caused deep sorrow to a wide circle of strongly attached friends. * *

Mr. Foster was a man of remarkable gifts as a writer and thinker. Had not his time been occupied with professional work he might have won distinction in literature. He was an amiable friend, and an affectionate husband and father. He leaves a sorrowing wife and two children to mourn his unexpected death. His funeral was largely attended by the clergy, and the bench and bar of the city. Mrs. Foster and the bereaved family have our deep sympathy in their great sorrow.

Monetary Times (Nov. 2, 1888).

A valuable life ended last night, when William A. Foster, Q.C., LL.B., passed away, valuable not only for what he had done, but for the possibilities of good work which lay before him. He was a true Canadian, a charming writer, a very able lawyer, and it is sad in many respects that he has been taken away in the very prime of his usefulness, for he was only 48 years of age. Years ago, with Thomas Moss, Wm. Rattray, A. C. Tyner, who are all dead, and a group of others who are still living, Mr. Foster did much to promote the growth of a distinctly Canadian feeling. His eloquent pamphlet, " Canada First," betrays a glow of patriotism, a pride of race, which could scarcely be believed to exist by those who later only knew the quiet, laborious lawyer. The deceased gentleman held for some years the important position of Canadian correspondent of the London *Times*, and filled it well. He was one of the founders of *The Monetary Times*, and was its first editor. Recognizing as he did the necessity for a journal that would, while avoiding the acridness and bias of ordinary political writing, devote honest criticism to commercial and political affairs, he established an independence of tone which it has been the aim of his successors to maintain.

Toronto Saturday Night (Nov. 10, 1888).

It was fitting that flowers should have covered the grave of that kindly gentleman and able lawyer, W. A. Foster. Beneath his easy and careless exterior were the impulses of a poet, the merriment of a humorist, the warmth of a generous and hospitable friend. Loyal alike to his clients and companions, no one spoke ill of him, and he never spoke ill of others. Malice and jealousy had no part in his noble nature, and all of us who knew him are saddened by the thought that we will see him no more. As a citizen, he was honest and patriotic; as a lawyer, he was always great and growing in fame; as a husband, he well deserved the love that will not forget him; as a son, his devotion had an exalted beauty, which perhaps best marks the tenderness and purity of his nature. As a *littérateur* he would have achieved eminence, and when he turned his attention to law Canadian letters suffered a lasting loss. The sorrowing friends who followed him to his grave brought flowers which softened by their loveliness the awfulness of death, and their perfume was a fitting emblem of the sweet memory—which will live, at least, as long as this generation lasts—of the lovable man we shall meet in office and street no more.

Canadian Methodist Magazine (December, 1888).

It is with the profoundest feelings of personal loss that we record the death of our early companion and life-long friend, the late W. A. Foster, Q C. By his death his profession loses a distinguished ornament and society a useful member; but to those who enjoyed his personal friendship the loss is one which cannot be expressed in words. He not only commanded their admiration for his intellectual abilities, but he was also endeared by his amiable qualities. We may not allow the public utterance of our personal sorrow, which is of too tender and sacred a character for record here.

INDEX.

	PAGE
Prefatory Note	iii
Introduction, by Mr. Goldwin Smith	1
Canada First : An Address	13
Address of the Canadian National Association	48
Address to the Canadian National Association	57
Party *versus* Principle. [*Daily Telegraph*]	87
The Canadian Confederacy. [*Westminster Review*]	93
The Canadian Confederation and the Reciprocity Treaty. [*Westminster Review*]	139
Down the St. Lawrence on a Raft. [*Canadian Monthly*]	169
The Late Adam Clarke Tyner. [*Daily Telegraph*, Oct. 25th, 1867]	199

IN MEMORIAM : Tributes called forth by Mr. Foster's death :

Mr. G. Mercer Adam, in *The Week*	201
Mr. Henry J. Morgan, in the *Ottawa Citizen*	206
Mr. Charles Mair's Poem, in *The Week*	210
The Mail	212
The Globe	214
The Empire	215
The World	216
The Daily News	217
Evening Telegram	218
Christian Guardian	219
Monetary Times	219
Saturday Night	220
Methodist Magazine	221

www.ingramcontent.com/pod-product-compliance
Lightning Source LLC
Chambersburg PA
CBHW030111030726
47498CB00007B/2334